MW00625875

FORGIVEN BY THE HERO

HEROES OF FREEDOM RIDGE

TARA GRACE ERICSON

Forgiven by the Hero
The Heroes of Freedom Ridge Book Six
Copyright © 2020 Tara Grace Ericson and Silver Fountain Press
All Rights Reserved

No part of this book may be used or reproduced in any manner
whatsoever without written permission, except in the case of brief
quotations embedded in critical articles and reviews. The unauthorized
reproduction or distribution of this copyrighted work is illegal. No part
of this book may be scanned, uploaded or distributed via the Internet or
any other means, electronic or print, without the author's permission.
This book is a work of fiction. The names, characters, places, and
incidents are products of the writer's imagination or have been used
fictitiously and are not to be construed as real. Any resemblance to
persons, living or dead, actual events, locale or organizations is entirely
coincidental. The author does not have any control over and does not
assume any responsibility for third-party websites or their content.
Published in the United States of America

Cover Designer: Amanda Walker PA & Design Services

Ebook ISBN: 978-1-949896-16-9
Paperback ISBN: 978-1-949896-17-6

✺ Created with Vellum

CONTENTS

To all the K9 Heroes working to keep us safe

Some trust in chariots and some in horses, but we trust in the name of the LORD our God.

— PSALM 20:5

1

*D*erek scanned the grey and brown landscape for any flash of color or movement. The hikers had been expected back yesterday afternoon but never showed up for their dinner reservation and were unreachable by cell phone according to the staff at Freedom Ridge Resort. It was now early in the morning, and Derek and a handful of other officers were scouring the hiking trails around the resort. It wasn't the first time vacationers had found themselves too far from the trail, and he was sure it wouldn't be the last.

Liberty sniffed nearby, staying close and showing no sign that she caught any trace of the missing hikers. Libby had been with him for four years, and the sweet German Shepherd was one of the best search and rescue dogs he'd ever trained.

His radio beeped and he heard the voice of Heath, the security guard at the resort. "Any sign of them, D?" While officers and park rangers were out searching, Heath was their central contact.

Derek pushed the button on the radio clipped near his collar and tipped his head to speak into the mic. "Nothing out here. I'm going to head about another mile west and see if they found their way down the ravine." Inexperienced hikers were far more likely to trek downhill, so the ravine would be a safe bet.

"10-4. I'll say a prayer."

"Anything from the team Northeast of the resort?"

"Nothing. But their family said they might have been headed for Freedom Falls."

That would have been nice to know earlier. "Thanks, Heath. I'm headed that way." Freedom Falls was a set of cascading waterfalls, especially in the spring when the snow was melting. But right now, they'd be mostly dry.

He spoke the command for Liberty to heel, and she turned quickly to find her place at his side. "Let's go, girl. We've got some tourists to find."

Fifteen minutes later, he found a rockslide blocking the well-marked trail. If the hikers had come this way, he'd bet this is where they left the marked trail. Liberty would find out. He grabbed the shirt Casey had given him, retrieved from the hikers' room and held it out to her. Liberty buried her nose in the fabric and then lowered her snout to the ground, sniffing around the edge of the fallen rock and then leading off the trail.

Liberty was a trailing dog; he'd taught her to follow a given scent track from the time she was barely six months old. After he left the army, where he worked with the dogs trained in all manner of things, he brought those skills home and started his own business. Now, DK9 Security bred and trained some of the most specialized working dogs in the country, right here in Freedom, Colorado.

He followed Liberty, careful to stay behind her and not contaminate the scent path she was tracking. If she found the source of the scent and Derek was too far behind, she would bark until he located her. Another skill he'd taught her.

The path led slowly downhill, as he suspected, and if they followed it long enough they would reach the ravine. He said a quick prayer for the hikers. It could be a treacherous forest, especially in the dark, and he hoped their delay was nothing serious. A thousand tragic scenarios could play out in the woods, just like whatever had happened to his sister all those years ago.

He carefully stepped under branches of the cedar and pine trees, and dry needles crunched under his boots. Rocks jutted up, threatening to roll an ankle or trip him if he wasn't careful with each footfall. He checked his GPS watch, verifying they'd gone one mile off the path now. He continued to follow Liberty, about a hundred yards ahead of him now.

His radio beeped and crackled. "Derek, check in?"

"Hey, Heath. Libby is onto something. We're about a mile off the Freedom Falls trail. A rockslide is blocking the trail, and I think they got lost trying to find a way around it."

He glanced ahead to where Libby showed no sign of losing the trail. "I think I'll find them. Have Carson ready for medical in case they need it.

"10-4. Keep us posted."

Thirty minutes and two miles later, Derek heard

Liberty's bark signaling from ahead of him. He couldn't fight the grin that broke across his face, and he rubbed a gloved hand over his beard. If Libby found them, there would be no unanswered questions. He hated the rare cases when a disappearance couldn't be explained. Like his sister's.

It took him a couple minutes to catch up, but he found Liberty standing at attention barking every few seconds at two people sitting on a rock and trying to shush her. He called a silence command to Liberty, and she stopped barking but stayed with the hikers. They turned toward him, and he held up a hand in greeting.

"James and Lisa Schomberg?" he asked once he was close enough.

They nodded, and Lisa wiped tears from her eyes. "Oh, thank God!" She buried her face in her husband's shoulder.

"I'm Derek Held, and this here is Liberty. We've been looking for you."

James held out a hand to shake his, and Derek saw the grimace of pain as his weight shifted. "Thanks. I screwed up my ankle pretty bad, I'm afraid. Then we weren't sure which way the trail was and didn't want to separate."

Derek smiled to reassure him. "It's alright. You did just fine." Now wasn't the time to lecture them about staying on the marked trail. "Now, let me take a look at that ankle."

$\sim$

MEGAN WARREN PULLED off Interstate 70 after driving an hour through Denver traffic and then another 90 minutes west of the city. The sign read "Freedom," and she hoped it would deliver. She would spend the next three months in a cabin in the Rockies. Marcus Warner needed to deliver another best-selling thriller to fans next year, and since she was Marcus Warner, it was her neck on the line.

The pressure never seemed to disappear, even after her first three novels had topped the charts and landed her on the tables right in front at every big bookstore across the country. Marcus Warner, best-selling author, had a certain ring to it. It would only be better if it could have been Megan Warren on the cover, but that wouldn't work for a myriad of different reasons.

No one outside of her immediate family knew that she was Marcus Warner, and she had to keep it that way. She would spend the next three months holed up in a picturesque cabin with a mountain view, writing the next book before she went home for Christmas. It was perfect.

The stone sign with metallic letters greeted her as the speed limit changed and the mountain highway carried into the small tourist town. Welcome to Freedom. The town was charming, pumpkins and straw bales with cute scarecrows graced doorsteps and store windows. She drove around the town square, with a courthouse in the middle and a large gazebo in the courtyard.

She spotted a couple of promising restaurants, though she planned to pick up groceries for the cabin and do most of her cooking. It would be a stretch, though since she usually relied on takeout along with frozen pizzas. Megan glanced at the time. She was supposed to meet

Pete for the key in an hour. That gave her some time to explore.

She pulled her rental car into a parking spot on a shop-lined street and got out to walk. The air was brisk, and far dryer than the humidity of the southern Alabama September she'd left behind. It actually felt like fall here, and she tugged her jacket a little tighter around her middle.

Megan wasn't ready to sit down yet, but a coffee shop caught her eye. When she stepped in the door, the familiar scents of coffee, cinnamon, and old books made her stop and drink it in. This might actually be heaven.

"Welcome to Stories and Scones!" a friendly voice called from behind the counter and Megan spotted a short-haired older woman fixing a drink behind the counter. Her smile was broad and inviting and Megan couldn't help but return it as she stepped closer to the counter.

After talking her into a house-specialty pumpkin spice latte, the woman introduced herself as Jan and got her name in return.

"How long are you in town for?"

"Until Christmas," Megan admitted.

"Wow, how wonderful!" Jan said. She reached for a pastry from the display case and handed it to Megan. When she held up a hand to protest, Jan set it in front of her. "On the house. Judging by your reaction to this place, I have a feeling I'll be seeing you a lot more while you're in Freedom."

"I'm staying in a cabin, actually. Do you know Pete O'Rourke?"

"Petey? Sure! Everyone knows Petey. His office is just down the way," Jan pointed to show her. "His cabins are the best. A bit of a trek from town, but you'll be comfortable.

That's exactly what Megan had been going for. This wasn't a survival test or an off-the-grid adventure. She needed wi-fi and hot showers. She'd leave the crazy back-woods adventures for her characters.

"Well, thanks for the scone."

"I'll see you around, Megan," Jan replied before disappearing into the kitchen.

Megan glanced around, debating between the small tables near the windows or the rows of bookshelves in the back of the store. Books would always win, so she wandered toward them. She might have to reward herself with a book as she hit certain milestones on her project. Afterall, one of the most important jobs of an author was to read books and refill the creative well.

Of course, she'd been doing that for months with nothing to show for it. Better not buy any books right now. She had her own story swirling around in her head and the most important thing for these two months was to get it down on paper. She took her latte and continued her stroll through Freedom.

Megan found the place where she was supposed to meet Petey, only four shops down from Stories and Scones. O'Rourke Insurance Agency was a simple business front with a green awning and a beautifully decorated front window. When she opened the door, a bell chimed. Moments later, an athletically-built man with salt-and-pepper hair and a button-down shirt came from an office in the back.

He held out his hand and said, "You must be Megan."

"And you must be Petey?" she replied as she shook it.

He laughed, "I see you met Jan. She's the only one who still calls me that. Childhood nicknames never die if you live in the same small town you always have."

Megan smiled, "Pete then. I'm excited to see the cabin."

Pete pulled out a drawer from the empty receptionist desk. "Everything should be ready for you." He handed her a stack of papers with a keychain on top. "Here's a map and your key and everything else you might need. Usually, I suggest people grab a drink at Jan's and look it over, but if you haven't eaten, might I recommend La Cresta? They've got the best tacos in The Rockies."

"Perfect, thanks so much!"

"My cell number is in there if you need anything. The cleaning service will come once a week while you stay, unless you call me and tell me not to send them."

"Okay. Best place to buy groceries?" Tacos sounded great for lunch, but she'd need something for dinner.

"In the packet," he tapped the papers he'd given her with a wink.

There was something reassuring about how clearly Pete had done this a hundred times before. She knew from the website that he had several of these cabins. But her imagination could run wild with a hundred scenarios, and she'd been tempted to stick with the larger, more expensive Freedom Ridge Resort. So many people would have driven her crazy, and she was looking forward to the silence and solitude of her remote cabin.

2

*M*egan carefully followed the printed directions from Pete's handy folder and turned off the winding state highway onto a narrow gravel drive that disappeared into the woods. Cedar and ash trees towered on either side of the drive, finally leading into a small clearing where the cabin sat. It looked just like the pictures she'd seen online, and a thrum of satisfaction rippled through her. Megan was a planner, and she had every detail of this trip planned to the very last pair of jeans in her suitcase.

It would have thrown everything off to discover the cabin was less than expected. Leaving the rest of her things in the car for now, Megan grabbed the bag of ice cream from the groceries. She slipped her finger through the key ring, letting it dangle happily from her hand as she stepped across the quiet clearing and up the porch steps to her temporary home. The porch was nice, but it looked to the woods, when she knew the view she would want to appreciate was on the back of the house.

She unlocked and opened the front door and was rewarded with the promised mountain view, a striking picture through large windows at the back of the house. To her right sat the kitchen, open to the rest of the living area. A wooden staircase led to the loft where she knew a simple desk would be sitting near a cozy sofa.

The cabin smelled like cedar wood and lemon scented cleaning products. Slowly, Megan wandered through the cozy space, trailing her fingertips on the counters and across the rough hewn mantle above the wood-burning fireplace. A short hallway led back to the only bathroom and bedroom.

To her disappointment, there was no bathtub. But the shower was spacious and the tile gleamed. She poked her head into the bedroom and the queen size bed that dominated the space. Yes, this would do nicely.

Her main character, Jett Winters, was due for another blood-racing adventure. And this peaceful hideaway was the perfect place for her to write it into existence.

She finished unloading her suitcases, packing everything into the dresser of the bedroom and neatly tucking the empty bags in the corner of the closet. Megan unloaded groceries and fixed herself dinner, then slowly climbed the stairs to the loft and sat at the old, wooden desk with a view of the mountain in front of her.

Brainstorming was her favorite phase of a project, and she set up her computer. A fresh notebook and three pens were placed neatly beside the closed laptop. As was often the case for her, Megan needed everything to be in place in order to work. It was one reason she usually found a place to hide from her life while she wrote. Interruptions from friends and family meant a break in her focus, and she couldn't afford that. A two-hour unplanned visit from a friend could throw off her writing schedule for a week.

Here, that wouldn't be an issue. Her cell reception was spotty, and the cabin had a landline. But it wasn't like she was going to call anyone. Her family knew she would be here until Christmas. She'd spend the next three months with her favorite man--Jett. He took the risks she couldn't and went on adventures she could only dream of.

She jotted down a daily schedule for herself. Early morning writing and a mid-morning walk to break up the day. She did want to enjoy the picturesque town of Freedom and maybe even venture to the lodge resort. Megan wouldn't be skiing, that was a bit too extreme. But it might be fun to watch other people do it. Maybe there would be a mountain setting in her book this time. In the last book, Jett traipsed across Europe in pursuit of a rogue agent and assassin plotting against the government. Perhaps it was time for a powerful shadow organization to threaten the global economy with some sort of crisis.

THE FOLLOWING WEEK, Derek watched with pride as Thor followed the path he'd laid yesterday, using the unique scent combinations he made himself. Thor excelled during the basic obedience training and now, at 6 months old, he was well mannered and eager to please, if still a little excitable at times.

The puppy stopped, confused by the spot where he had doubled back. Derek was rooting for him, but stood by, waiting for Thor to lead the way. He sniffed around, located the other path and led Derek down the trail.

With a practiced motion, Derek unclipped the lead and let Thor follow the remaining trail to the small, hollowed out tree where he'd hidden a strong scent origin and the pup's reward—a chew toy with peanut butter. When he heard Thor barking, he smiled. Derek hadn't expected him to remember that part without prompting. Thor's barking grew more excited, and he frowned. That didn't sound right.

Then he heard the laughter. Rounding the corner, he saw Thor spinning eagerly in front of a woman who was currently laughing and showering him with affection. Thor's tail was wiggling uncontrollably, moving the puppy's entire back half.

Derek gave the command, and Thor instantly turned and ran toward him with an excited leap. He heard a soft exclamation of surprise from the woman.

"He's a beautiful dog," she called. Derek didn't reply. He rewarded Thor with a treat from his pocket, then held out the scented rag again, with the command to find. Thor needed to finish his task. Then, Derek would deal with the woman in his woods.

"I'm sorry, I didn't realize--" Derek held up a hand in a 'stop' motion, hoping she would understand.

Thor pushed his nose to the ground and finished his search, uncovering the peanut butter toy. It was frustrating that Thor had lost focus so close to the end of the search. The dog loved people, and the hardest part of his training would be teaching him to ignore everyone but Derek and everything but the task at hand. Derek patted the dog and pushed the button on the clicker he used to reinforce praise. He ignored the feeling of being watched.

She hadn't come any closer, but the woman watched Thor curiously, a smile playing on her lips. Her brown hair was pulled back into a low ponytail and her thick-framed glasses seemed to overwhelm her round face. Who was she?

Finally, he knew he had to speak. Truthfully, she'd done nothing wrong except happen upon his little training exercise. The fact that this was Thor's biggest task yet and Derek had spent two hours walking this same trail yesterday in preparation wasn't her fault. "Sorry about that. Thor is training, and he needed to finish his job." Derek took a few steps, climbing the stairsteps of rocks leading to her position on higher ground.

"Oh, I didn't mean to interrupt. I can go," she said, turning back and pointing the other way.

"It's okay. He's done now. I just didn't expect to see anyone. These are private woods and not a lot of hikers come out this way." That was an understatement. Pete O'Rourke owned nearly half the mountain and most of his renters never went nearly this far away from the cabins. She didn't answer right away, and Derek heard alarm bells in his head.

He hated being lied to. After his sister disappeared, his parents had spiraled into a life of drugs and alcohol, complete with excuses and lies to their sixteen-year-old son. They stole his cash, humiliated him in front of his peers and teachers, and made him wary of trusting anyone again.

He knew his habit of holding people at arm's length

wasn't exactly healthy, but it was the best defense he had. If he let people get too close, they could take advantage of him. Or worse, make him care and be unable to help when they needed it.

~

MEGAN DEBATED HOW TO RESPOND. She didn't know anything about this man, other than he had an adorable puppy and was apparently training him for something. Should she tell him where she was staying? That seemed unwise. She was, after all, a woman living in the woods alone.

"I rented a cabin nearby." Hopefully that was vague enough to keep him from finding her, but explained her presence. "Am I not supposed to be in this part of the woods?"

He shook his head. "No, it's fine. Pete lets me bring the dogs out here. I guess you're in one of his cabins?"

Megan nodded. So much for anonymity. "I'm Megan."

"Derek."

"Nice to meet you, Derek. And nice to meet you, Thor." She directed her comment toward his feet where the energetic puppy was pouncing on some sort of toy. The dog had come out of nowhere, interrupting her walk. She'd been in Freedom for three days, and while she'd written a little, she was still in the planning phases for her book. A walk sounded like the perfect way to clear her head and get the creative juices flowing. It had, until a forty-pound ball of fur had run straight into her ankles.

Thor's owner was certainly interesting. His piercing

blue eyes studied her, and she wanted to squirm under the scrutiny. Derek looked far more comfortable in the woods in his cargo pants and red windbreaker than she probably did in her jeans and hoodie. His dark beard completed the mountain man look, and she couldn't help but wonder if he ever wore plaid flannel shirts.

"Sorry he interrupted your hike. He should have been able to ignore you."

Well, that seemed kind of insulting. "Oh, he was just saying hello."

Derek huffed a breath. "He should have been working. That's his job. If he had been looking for a missing person and a hiker distracted him, the trail could be lost entirely. Thor will need to learn how to shut out the distractions."

Whoa. This guy took the job of a puppy pretty seriously. "So, what? He doesn't get to be a puppy?"

Derek pointed to Thor, and Megan followed with her eyes. The dog was happily rolling around in the dirt with the chew toy in his mouth. "Does he look miserable to you? Overworked?"

Megan smiled as she watched the puppy enjoy his prize. "I guess not. I'm sorry I implied that. It's not my place. I should go." She turned and headed back down the trail toward her cabin.

"How long are you staying?" Derek's deep voice called after her.

"Long enough," was the only answer she gave in return.

3

Three days after Thor's big test took an unexpected turn, Derek finished some paperwork, then ran some team drills with Thor and Libby with Jared, his co-trainer. He finished some paperwork then headed out to grab a cup of coffee. Stepping into Stories and Scones, he spotted Jan laughing with Pete O'Rourke at the end of the bar.

"Hey, stranger," Jan greeted him. "About time you showed up. Aiden said he hasn't seen you much." Aidan was one of his closest friends and was a firefighter and snowboard instructor. Aiden married Joanna earlier this year, and it had seriously cut into their hang out time.

"I'll give him a call."

"What have you been up to? I feel like I barely see Aiden and Jo, let alone his friends."

Derek smiled. He was happy for his friend, and he really did like Joanna as well. She fit right in their little town. "That's good. I've got a litter of puppies almost ready to graduate, so I'm keeping pretty busy." Derek glanced at Pete, "Speaking of which, I met your current renter the other day on one of my training exercises. Quiet thing, kind of nervous. I wish I'd known you had someone staying there right now. I'd have postponed until they were gone."

"Sorry, Derek. I didn't even think about it. But I don't think postponing would work. She's here until Christmas."

His eyebrows twitched. What kind of person rented an expensive mountain cabin like that for three entire months? Pete's cabins were usually rented a week at a time at the most. Usually just on the weekends, except around the holidays.

"Wow. I guess I'll keep that in mind if I need to use the mountain."

"You've got the number for the cabins, right? She's in the Cedar Crest Cabin."

"Is that the one north of the highway?"

"Yeah, the smaller one," Pete confirmed.

Interesting. That meant Megan was at least a couple miles from her cabin when Thor found her. She wasn't dressed like a hiker, so what was she doing? He couldn't deny the fact that he was curious about her. A beautiful woman wandering the woods alone and staying for months in a mountain cabin? It wasn't exactly behavior he saw every day.

The bells on the door chimed and Derek turned to see the familiar brown eyes he hadn't been able to forget in three days. Did they really hold as many secrets as he imagined? Or was he letting his suspicious nature take over?

It was no surprise that Jan was the first to greet the visitor in a cheerful voice. "Welcome back! I hope Petey's cabin is treating you well."

"Hi, Jan," Megan replied quietly, ducking her head. "Pete, good to see you again."

Pete smiled broadly. "I hear you ran into Derek here out on the mountain the other day. I hope one of his dogs didn't scare you too badly."

Derek resisted the urge to roll his eyes. His dogs never scared anyone.

"Sorry I didn't warn you about him. It's private property, but I let Derek and Jared use it for training. It's more than worth it to know we have the best trained search and rescue dogs available if we ever need them."

She shook her head, "It was no problem for me."

Derek pulled off his hat. "Can I buy you a cup of coffee and make it up to you?" He wanted to get to know her a little better, see what was making his spidey-sense tingle. It didn't hurt that she was the first woman in ten years to make his pulse jump and his breath shaky.

Her gaze flew to his eyes at the question, confusion etched on her face. Had he been that gruff on the mountain?

"Umm, I guess," she replied.

Jan busied herself fixing drinks and then gave Derek a wide-eyed look of glee and encouragement when he grabbed them from her at the end of the bar. Aidan's mom had been as much a mother to him as anyone, since his own family left much to be desired in the parent department. He tried to convey a silent plea of "Chill out, it's just coffee," with his eyes but he could already see her planning another wedding in her mind.

Megan was waiting at one of the small bistro tables across from the coffee bar, her jacket slung over the back of the chair. He studied her for a moment. Unlike most people he watched, she didn't fidget or obsessively glance at her phone. She simply sat, still and stoic. As he neared the table, she gave another small smile and adjusted her chair slightly.

"I got you a Ridge Top Mocha. Jan said you hadn't tried one yet. It's the house specialty," he added awkwardly. Shaking his head to clear it, he pulled out his own chair and sat down.

"So, how is Thor?" Megan asked with her hands cupped around the outside of the mug.

The smile that pulled on his lips was pure reflex. Thor, and his littermates, were one of his most promising cohorts yet. "He's doing great. When he's done with training and assessments, Thor will be a top-notch SAR dog."

"SAR dog?"

"Search and Rescue. It's important up here on the mountain, but Thor could end up anywhere across the country. I train bomb-detecting dogs and drug dogs, too."

"Whoa. That's pretty incredible."

He shrugged. Once you knew how to train a dog, the different types of training weren't all that different. But his passion was for SAR dogs who could follow a trail. He could never shake the idea that if the teams looking for his sister had dogs with them, they might have found her.

"Where are you from? That accent... Somewhere south, I gather?"

She smiled, "Alabama, born and raised."

"How do you like Freedom so far? First time here?"

"Yep, first time. It's beautiful. Pete's cabin is nice, and I love the mountain."

He couldn't resist the temptation to dig further. "Pete mentioned you would be here until Christmas. That's a lot longer than most of our visitors."

She shrugged and looked down at her coffee. "I'm working on a project and need the solitude." Then, she glanced up and toward the books, "Want to take a look around the book section? I could use a book out at the cabin."

What he wanted was to continue asking questions, but he knew when to stop. "Sure."

They wandered through the books, and Derek skimmed the titles until he found the one he wanted. Marcus Warner was his newest favorite author. The Jett Winters series was like watching a Hollywood action flick, without the swear words. He grabbed a copy of the book that had come out just a few weeks ago. "Oh good. I've been wanting to pick this up."

She turned toward him to look, and he held it up. Megan choked on her drink and started to cough. When she had cleared her throat, she apologized. "Sorry, wrong pipe. That looks...manly," she finished.

He laughed. "I suppose it is. He writes these super intense action adventures. It's the best. I'd say he's my favorite author right now."

～

UNABLE TO HIDE HER SURPRISE, Megan turned and grabbed a book off the shelf. What were the odds that this gorgeous, slightly intimidating man would be a fan of her writing? The logical side of her brain started actually doing the calculations based on what she knew of her sales and demographics, but she forced herself to stop. It didn't matter what the odds were. The important part was escaping from this conversation as quickly as possible without blowing her cover. She couldn't let Derek know that she was Marcus Warner. She skimmed the cover of the book she held, feeling the heat rise in her cheeks when she saw she'd grabbed another one of her own books.

"Hmmm, looks interesting," she choked out, still clearing her throat from the inhalation of her drink a moment ago. Then, she slid it back on the shelf and moved on to another section. She grabbed a mystery paperback and held it up. "I'll stick with this for now."

"Your loss. Even Joanna likes Jett Winters."

Joanna? He spoke the name with so much fondness, Megan glanced at his left hand to be sure. No ring, but that didn't always mean he wasn't married. Maybe they were just dating. Or maybe she was his sister.

She shook her head to clear it. Whoever Joanna was, it didn't matter because she was Megan Warren and Marcus Warner, and she was only in Freedom Ridge until Christmas. No matter how charming Derek was or how cute his dog was.

Megan made a show of glancing at her watch and claiming she needed to get back, then quickly paid Jan for her book. As Derek paid for a copy of the book she'd written last year and edited earlier this year, she hastily said goodbye. "Thanks for the coffee. I'll try to stay away from your training grounds."

When she stepped out of the restaurant and safely on the sidewalk, Megan took a deep breath. That was close. She didn't like to lie, and the penname had been more of a necessity than anything else. She couldn't afford to let her true name come out though. With the success of her books, it would likely be front page news, and that would mean Tristan would be able to find her. She shivered, not entirely from the brisk October day.

Tristan had started as a friend in college. First, he was in a few of her classes senior year. Then, his entire schedule matched hers, and he spent every moment hanging around the coffee shop where she worked. When she'd tried to reject his advances, he hadn't taken it well. He continued to harass and stalk her after graduation, finally discouraged by a restraining order followed by her complete disappearance from social media. He would have to work awfully hard to find her again, since she paid a good sum of money to a security firm in Birmingham to keep her information unlisted.

If it came out that she was Marcus Warner, though? All bets were off, and Tristan could show up again. It could easily be another fan, too. She was grateful her publisher had understood her concerns. Besides, action thrillers were predominantly written by men anyway, it made sense to use a fake name.

As Megan drove back to her cabin, she prayed about it. She wanted to be honest with Derek, but she also wanted to protect herself. She needed wisdom. And she really needed to shake off the surprises of this afternoon and focus on writing.

Jett Winters couldn't disappoint Derek when he read the next Marcus Warner novel.

4

$\mathcal{M}$egan was making good progress on her book. After three weeks in Freedom, she had planned her novel and was working through the first draft. Jett had already gotten himself embroiled in a global conspiracy, and he was the only one who could get himself out.

When she emerged from the loft after a marathon writing session, Megan heard the howl of a dog outside her door. With a frown, she peeked through the pane-glass window near the kitchen and saw a German Shepherd puppy whining at the door. Was it Thor?

She opened the door and the puppy cowered at her legs, rolling over and displaying its belly. Megan obliged the poor thing with pats and belly rubs and then called for it to follow her back outside. If this was one of Derek's dogs, surely he wouldn't be too far behind.

Instead of taking to the woods to search, Megan waited in one of the Adirondack chairs on the front porch and watched the treeline for a familiar flash of the red jacket Derek always seemed to be wearing.

As she waited, she played with the dog. The tag on the pup's collar said "Dobby," and she snorted when she recognized the reference to Harry Potter, which was one of her favorite series. Dobby sat next to her and whined if Megan stopped petting her. This puppy definitely had the loyalty of a house elf.

About fifteen minutes, Megan went inside to grab her phone. The signal was spotty, but maybe she could get a text out to Pete so he could let Derek know where his dog was. She sent the message and waited. It looked like it had gone through.

Twenty minutes after that, a navy-blue Jeep Cherokee pulled up the drive and parked next to her rental car. A shield logo emblazoned on the door read "DK9 Security," and her pulse accelerated as Derek stepped down from the vehicle.

Dobby was apparently just as excited to see Derek as Megan was and immediately took off toward his owner. He knelt down to give the dog attention and then stood and walked toward her.

"I think your dogs like me," she said by way of greeting.

"Thanks for getting a hold of Pete. Dobby here took off after a deer earlier, and the leash snapped. Libby and I have been looking for her for a couple of hours."

She grimaced, "Yikes. Glad he found me, I guess. Care to take a seat?"

"Sure. Let me let Libby out of the truck, though."

Megan watched as Derek returned to the truck and

opened the back seat. A gorgeous adult German Shepherd leapt gracefully from the backseat, wearing a red Search Dog vest. Dobby ran up to her, but Libby stayed close to Derek until he released her with a wave of his hand and the word "Free."

Then, he collapsed in the chair next to her.

"Coffee?"

He didn't answer right away. "That sounds like heaven."

Megan went inside and made two cups of coffee with the sleek single-cup brewing station. When she carried them out to the porch, Derek was watching Libby and Dobby playing in the grass, picking up sticks and wrestling over them.

"Here you go. I hope black is okay."

"That's perfect."

Dobby came back to the porch and sat expectantly in front of Derek. He tried to wave him away, but Dobby only shifted to be in front of Megan. "Who's a good boy?"

In response, Dobby started letting out little howling noises. Megan mimicked the dog, "ahhoooh, aooooh," while laughing at the dog's antics.

Derek hurriedly tried to shush Megan, "No, don't—" but then Dobby has already taken the encouragement and was standing on his hind legs, still singing and doing a dance. Megan burst into laughter and Derek hung his head in his hands. "My friend Haven has a little girl, Miah. Dobby spent the weekend with them and came back singing."

Megan was still cracking up at the performance from

the adorable German Shepherd and replied, "That's hysterical!"

Derek gave Dobby a command to be down and grumbled, "It's embarrassing, actually. I don't think Dobby's going to cut it as a working dog, but I haven't had the heart to officially flunk him."

"You're like the mean teacher in school who is secretly kind and mushy."

"I am *not* mushy," Derek replied with mock horror, and Megan laughed again.

"Whatever you say, Professor."

Dobby went back to wrestle with Libby and they sat in comfortable silence for a few moments before Derek spoke. "I haven't seen you around town much. Have you done anything except work on your project?"

She shook her head. "Not really."

"I could show you around a bit, make sure you get the full Freedom Ridge experience."

"I don't know... I'm more of a homebody."

"I already know you like to hike a little. How about we go see Freedom Falls? It's supposed to rain this weekend and warm up on Monday. I bet we could catch them flowing if we time it right."

Megan had seen Freedom Falls mentioned in Pete's trusty book. The picture was stunning, and she would like to see it. But she probably shouldn't hike alone. She nodded, "Okay. That sounds like fun."

Derek's smile was bright and caught her by surprise. He was so serious most of the time. "I'll call you and let you know when. It'll depend on when the rain stops."

Sunday night, Megan watched the billowing storm

clouds roll in over the mountains through the big window she liked to sit in front of and brainstorm. When she was writing, Megan preferred the loft, with its small desk and smaller windows. If she found herself getting restless, pacing the cabin, she'd hike through the unfamiliar forest to clear her head and stretch her legs. Tonight though, the storm clouds made that a bad idea. Later, she listened to the thunderstorm and water pounding the cabin roof. An unfamiliar phone rang, and she looked around to locate the source of the sound.

"Hello?" She answered the landline hesitantly, unsure of who would be calling her. The storm and the dark giving distinct horror movie vibes to her solitude.

"Still on for a late autumn hike?" Derek's familiar voice rang clearly through the line, and she relaxed immediately.

"Yep," she replied.

"Alright. Tomorrow about eleven, okay? I'll meet you at the resort, and we can leave from there. Dress warm and in layers. I'll bring everything else."

Megan felt the excitement hum through her body. She wasn't this person. She didn't go for hikes to waterfalls that would only exist for a day before disappearing again. She didn't spend time with men she barely knew, either.

But for some reason, she wanted to do this. And she wanted to spend time with Derek. After laying out her clothes for tomorrow, Megan turned off the lights inside the cabin and watched the storm through the big windows, enjoying the show God was putting on with spectacular lightning.

5

*D*erek loaded Libby into the Jeep and slammed the door. The rain had died down around midnight, and he knew the falls would flow until late this afternoon before disappearing again. This was probably the last good rainfall of the year. If it had been a little cooler last night, that storm would have dumped six inches of snow. Today, though, it was a cool 45 degrees. The hike would keep them warm, though.

Plus, he was going to cheat a little and take Megan in his Jeep so they could cut the loop down to four miles, instead of the ten it would be from the lodge. He knew this mountain inside and out, and sometimes that knowledge had its advantages.

He parked near the entrance of Freedom Ridge Resort and saw Megan waiting by her car. Which begged another question--who rented a car for two entire months instead of driving her own car? What was this project, and how much did Megan get paid to work on it? He dismissed the questions and focused on enjoying the day. Even without his skeptical curiosity, Derek found himself interested in Megan. She was unique and confident. And yes, lovely with her soft curves and friendly smile. Her warm eyes invited him in each time he saw her.

She straightened as he approached and gestured to the lodge. "This place is incredible. I haven't had a chance to come see it yet."

Derek looked at the familiar lodge with fresh eyes. It was an impressive building with beautiful architecture and stunning views of the mountains. The restaurant inside, Liberty Grille, had really good food. Several of Derek's friends, including Aiden and Daniel, worked at the lodge and the tourism dollars definitely kept the businesses in town thriving year-round.

"We should be back in time for a late lunch if you want to grab it inside. It's probably all decked out for the fall." Hints of the decorations sat outside, straw bales and pumpkins and giant fall wreaths on the doors. But he knew from experience the inside would be a whole other level.

"Sounds good. I'm getting a little tired of cooking," she said with a chuckle.

He opened the door to his Jeep to let her inside. Megan turned and gave Libby a neck rub, and the dog nearly tried to climb up in her lap. They said dogs were good judges of character. Maybe he was being suspicious for no reason. They drove away from the lodge toward the small dirt road he knew would take them close to the trail.

It was a cold morning, and Derek was pleased to see Megan was dressed for the weather, smartly in layers she could remove as the day warmed. He let Liberty down from the truck and tightened the laces on his hiking boots as Megan played with the dog. Then they took off into the woods.

"I hope you know where you're going," Megan said from behind him, a hint of anxiety in her voice.

"Sure do. I keep all the bodies out here," he joked, with a mischievous grin back at her.

She glared at him. "Very funny."

They walked uphill, stepping over downed trees and carefully navigating rocks still slippery from last night's rain. They reached the main trail just minutes later.

"We took a bit of a short cut," Derek explained, pointing to the right. "Back there about three miles, is the resort. We've only got about two miles to the falls this way," he pointed to the left. "I figured on a cold day, five miles was plenty."

"That's great. I don't exactly do this every day. And back home, I do even less."

"What do you do for work, anyway?"

She hesitated, but he couldn't tell if it was because of the question or because she was stepping up a series of rocks on the trail. "Oh, I'm a writer."

A writer. That explained the solitary cabin. She must be a pretty successful one to afford it for so long. They continued for another thirty minutes until they came to one of Derek's favorite overlooks. From there, hikers could see the falls they were headed toward. When you took the longer hike all the way from the resort, by this point, you were tempted to turn around, until you saw the finish line. It was still a half-mile of trail away, down one ridge and up the other, but the view was stunning. He glanced at Megan to gauge her reaction.

"Wow," she breathed. They had timed it correctly and Freedom Falls was flowing, though not with the roaring waters of early spring.

He looked at the face of the woman beside him. She was enraptured by the view, and the morning light made her warm brown eyes look like honey.

"Beautiful," he murmured, still looking at her. When he realized he'd spoken out loud, Derek turned his gaze toward the falls. "Should we get a closer view?"

MEGAN FOLLOWED Derek and Libby down the narrow trail, huffing slightly as the trial began to slope upward again. Her day job as a freelance editor and her main gig as an author did not lend itself to physical fitness, a fact she was exceedingly aware of as she watched Derek tackle the climb as though it were a boardwalk stroll in Gulf Shores.

She stepped to the side and pulled off the zip up jacket she'd worn over two long sleeve shirts, tying it around her waist. Then she took a drink, adjusted the headband that covered her ears, and continued up the trail. She was strong, she could do this. For some reason, she felt the drive to prove to Derek that she wasn't the boring, straight-laced woman she was so used to being. In some ways, she was tired of letting Jett Winters have all the fun.

At least Derek hadn't pressed her on the issue of her writing.

Derek stopped at the top of a hill, and she came up beside him, the sound of falling water filling the small opening. Just across the small clearing, Freedom Falls was close enough to touch, and she started to step toward them. Derek held out an arm to stop her, "Be careful. It could be slippery after such a chilly morning."

With a nod of acknowledgment, she held his arm and then inched closer to the falling water, which cascaded over the rocks in front of her. The falls ended in a section of creek that was relatively flat and then continued down the hill.

"Thanks for bringing me here. I would never have seen it if it weren't for you."

"My pleasure. And," he glanced at his dog standing near the falls trying to bite the falling water, "obviously Liberty loves to come here, too."

Megan laughed at the dog's antics. "She is precious. How old is she?"

"Liberty is five. She was part of the first litter I ever bred for Search and Rescue. Been with me ever since." He gave a command and Libby ran toward him. Her obedience was amazing. "She's kind of a local hero. Over the last four years, Libby and I have found twenty-one missing hikers and one little girl who got lost in the woods."

Megan filled with awe at the work of the man standing next to her. "That's incredible."

He shrugged. "It's important. The dogs are amazing at what they do."

"I'm sure that's true. But they also have a good trainer."

Derek gave a low hum and then bent down to throw a

stick for Libby, effectively ending their conversation. After the hike back to the car, Megan was warm and sweaty, despite the cool mountain air.

Derek parked next to her car in the nearly empty Freedom Ridge Resort lot. "You hungry?"

"Famished."

He left the windows open for Libby and they walked in together. Inside the resort, Megan had to stop to admire the soaring ceiling of the great room and the large stone fireplace. The mantle was laden with autumn leaves, gourds, and candles in earthy colors. All throughout the lobby and lounge were elegant touches of fall.

"You'll have to come back once they've decorated for Christmas," Derek whispered.

"Derek, is that you?" A woman held up a hand across the lobby and headed toward them. Beside her, Derek gave the woman a brief hug.

"Haven, how are you? Is Jeremiah around?" He glanced at Megan, then chided himself. "Oh, I'm sorry. Haven, this is Megan. She's staying in one of Pete's cabins, and we hiked out to Freedom Falls this morning. Megan, this is Haven. Haven is the event coordinator around here, so she's basically the one who really runs things."

Megan laughed at his introduction and shook Haven's hand.

"Just don't tell Kevin," she said with a wink. "Nice to meet you, Megan. Jeremiah is around here somewhere. We'll see you at Carson's wedding, right Derek?"

"Wouldn't miss it," he said.

Haven leaned close to Derek and spoke in a stage

whisper, "Looks like you might even be able to bring a date for once, eh?"

Megan felt the heat rise in her cheeks. Haven was fun, but Megan hated that she was putting Derek on the spot like that.

"We better go," he said instead of responding. He stepped away from Haven and waved, "Worked up an appetite on that hike, you know." He tugged on Megan's hand when they had turned around to head into the restaurant, Megan saw the smile teasing at his lips.

"She seems nice," Megan said as the hostess seated them.

"Haven and Jeremiah are a bit like a second family to me. She's right, you know. I'd love to have you come to the wedding."

Instinctively, Megan shook her head. "Oh, no, you don't have to do that. Just because Haven said that, I'm--"

"I promise I wouldn't let Haven pressure me into something I didn't want. I think it's good for you to have some friends while you're here. It's got to be a bit lonely in that cabin by yourself."

Megan's heart sank. Friends, of course. Derek wanted to be her friend. That made perfect sense. Far more sense than him having a romantic interest in her. She was just getting caught up in the fun of a vacation romance. But she wasn't on vacation. Megan was here to work and she needed to remember that.

"I'm really fine. I should probably get back to that cabin pretty soon anyway and get back to work. I hope you have fun at the wedding though."

The remainder of lunch was slightly jilted and

awkward and Megan was happy to escape to her car and make the drive to her cabin. As homey and inviting as it was when she'd first walked in, today it did seem a little emptier.

She took a shower and went up to the loft. It would be a short writing day since she was worn out from the hike. Writing something seemed important right now, if only to remind herself why she was there. She glanced at the calendar above the small desk. There was a month until Thanksgiving and she still had a lot of work to do. Jett Winters was slowly unraveling the web of conspiracy, and it had him trekking across a mountain to a secret missile silo.

DEREK RESISTED the urge to scold Dobby as the dog, once again, veered off course to sniff at something off the trail. Instead, he gave the *search* command again and rewarded Dobby with a click when he jumped back on the trail. The dog was incredibly friendly and very fast. The stamina alone would make him an asset on long hikes or searches. But if Dobby didn't tone down some of the extracurriculars and figure out how to stay focused, he would be out of a job.

The woods were nice today, though much colder than his hike with Megan had been. He hadn't seen or heard from her in the two weeks since that day, and he was trying not to let it get to him. She was busy, right?

Just because he'd been tempted to kiss her by the waterfall didn't mean there was anything to get torn up about. No matter how much he wanted to accidentally bump into her in town again. Maybe Jan would send him a text the next time Megan stopped by Stories and Scones. Surely an author would visit the bookstore again soon. He winced. That seemed like a step too far. Almost stalkerish.

He thought about calling to see if she would be interested in going to the wedding. She'd seemed pretty adamant about not, though, and he wanted to respect that. He debated his options while he evaluated Dobby's accuracy on the trail he'd placed. Not bad, but not great.

Derek wanted to see Megan again, that much was clear. But how?

Dobby left the trail again and Derek groaned. "Dobby," he got the dog's attention. This wasn't going to work. But he wasn't ready to give up on the dog yet. And he wasn't ready to give up on Megan yet, either.

6

*D*erek finished the knot on his tie, then glanced in the mirror to straighten it. Less than a year ago, Carson and Nicole had been mere acquaintances, now they were getting married. It was kind of amazing how God could bring people together. Derek was pretty sure that wasn't in the cards for him though. God had called him to train rescue dogs and help people. And since he hadn't been able to help his sister all those years ago, it felt like the right thing to do.

Still, he hated going to weddings alone. Didn't everyone? Most of his friends had paired off over the last few years. Aiden and Joanna, Haven and Jeremiah. Even his grumpy buddy Daniel broke down and fell for the chef at the restaurant he managed. Now, it was just Derek and Max. He loved his friend from the local police department, but he could think of better-looking dates for this wedding.

Specifically a curvy brunette currently haunting his mountain and his daydreams. They'd had a great time on their hike to the falls, and it had been amazing to share the moment she first saw the view. But Megan had pulled back at the end of the day, and he hadn't heard from her since.

He shrugged on his suit jacket and patted his pockets to check for his wallet and the wedding card. Thankfully, Carson and Nicole had settled on a small event, otherwise Derek might have gotten roped into being in the wedding. Aiden was the best man. Carson Leavey was an EMT for the Fire Department, and Derek worked with him on rescue missions occasionally. Derek, Aiden, and Carson spent a lot of time together. Or used to before his buddies found love.

Once inside the familiar sanctuary at Freedom Bible Church, Derek grabbed a program and found a seat next to Max. The music played softly and the church was covered in flowers.

"Hey," he whispered. Max lifted his chin to return the greeting. "Reception is at the lodge, right?"

Max nodded, "Yeah, Haven pretty much insisted, even though ski season is in full swing."

Derek laughed softly. "Yeah, with that snow the other night, I bet Aiden is dying to get out on the mountain." Aiden was a snowboard instructor at the resort and a fire-fighter in town.

The music grew louder, and they twisted in their chairs to watch as the family was escorted to their rows in the front.

Carson took his place at the front of the church, followed by Aiden and the maid of honor, Addison. The music shifted and the minister asked them to rise. Derek looked toward the back of the church and caught a glimpse of Nicole. Then, unable to resist, he turned his gaze toward his friend waiting for his bride. Carson's face was an expression of pure adoration and a bit of disbelief and awe that Nicole was actually walking down the aisle toward him.

As the couple said their vows, Derek felt the knot in his throat, full of emotion at seeing his childhood friend pledging forever to the woman he loved. He was content with his friends and his dogs, but things like this had him wishing for someone to share life with. Just like Thanksgiving next week with Aiden and Joanna would make him wish his family wasn't the mess it was.

At the reception, Derek sat with his friend, Jeremiah, and his wife, Haven. Their daughter, Miah, kept asking when they could have cake, which had Derek holding back his laughter and earning good-natured scowls from Haven. Max filled him in on his most recent efforts to get the police department to spend the Christmas budget on a better coffee maker.

"I'm telling you, none of them have any taste buds or something."

"That's why those of us with sense still go see Jan at Stories and Scones way too often," Derek said.

The dance floor opened and he watched Carson and Nicole enjoy their first dance. Derek danced with Miah, letting her stand on his shoes as she held his fingers. Nearby, Aiden danced with Joanna. When the dance ended, Derek caught Joanna before she could leave the floor. "Mind if I get the next one?"

Jo wrapped him in a huge hug and grabbed his hand

for a dance. As they danced and talked, he squirmed as she studied his expression. "What's wrong, Derek?"

"Nothing at all. It was a beautiful ceremony, wasn't it?" Trying to deflect the conversation was unlikely to work on the woman who knew him better than nearly any other, but it was worth a shot.

"Nice try. I thought Jan said you were going to bring Megan?"

"I asked, but she turned me down." He didn't like how pathetic he sounded saying that, so he straightened his shoulders and added, "It's better this way. She's only in town for another month." He spun her under his arm and flashed a smile.

With that, Joanna allowed the subject change and started off on a story about the florist and the keys to the banquet room while they finished their dance. "Luckily, Haven came through at the last minute. That girl is a lifesaver. I'm so glad they ended up agreeing to have the reception here."

"Did you hear Haven has a baby on the way?"

Joanna nodded, "Yes! Miah is so excited to be a big sister."

Derek laughed, "And Jeremiah seems ready to wrap Haven in a giant sleeve of bubble wrap until the baby comes."

Derek escorted Joanna back to Aiden and then made his way back to his table, where he found Haven and Jeremiah chatting with Daniel and Ashley Winchester. The manager and chef of Liberty Grille had gotten married earlier this year, and Daniel had recently joined the men's

Bible study at church. It was nice to get to know him better over the last eight months.

"Hey Danny. Hey Ashley."

Always shy, Ashley barely met his eyes as she responded with a quiet, "Hello."

Haven perked up, "Derek, I was just telling them about the message you got about Ninja the other day."

He swelled with pride. Two years ago, he had trained Ninja as a bomb-detection dog. The handler who worked with Ninja now sent pictures of him screening luggage at the airport in Los Angeles.

He told the table about Ninja's accomplishments and enjoyed the rest of the evening. Derek knew he needed to focus on his dogs and forget about the woman hiding away on the mountain writing her romance novel. At least, that's what he assumed she was writing. She probably wrote sensitive, sappy dudes who wrote poetry or something. He knew he could be too serious and a bit grumpy. Joanna and Haven were always telling him so. Maybe that was why Megan hadn't wanted to come to the wedding. The thought pulled his mouth into a frown. The last thing he wanted was to scare Megan away. Quite the opposite, in fact.

---

7

*T*he following Thursday, Derek knocked on the door at Aiden and Joanna's house, balancing a pie he had special-ordered from Stories and Scones. Miah answered the door, a bundle of energy. "Guess what day it is, Uncle D!"

Derek pretended to be stumped. "Hmmm, is it Sunday?"

"No!" Miah protested with a fit of giggles.

"Is it Valentine's Day?" Miah gave him the kind of over-the-top eye roll only five-year-olds seemed to master.

"It's Thanksgiving!"

"Ohhhh," Derek feigned surprise. "Good thing I brought this pie, I guess!"

"Pie? Cool!" Miah said before running away and leaving Derek to step inside and shut the door behind him. In the kitchen, Joanna and Haven were chatting away with Jan.

"Derek! So glad you were able to come this year! Aiden and Jerm are watching the game in the living room."

He found his friends in front of the Broncos game. By the time dinner was ready and Aiden carved the turkey, the house was full of mouthwatering aromas and Derek was eager to dive in.

Aiden prayed over the food, and Derek filled with joy seeing the difference two years had made for his friend. When Derek moved to Freedom, he and Aiden had met on the slopes, but Aiden's faith had really solidified after meeting Joanna.

"This looks amazing, Jo," Derek said as he dished himself a hearty scoop of mashed potatoes before passing them to Aiden.

"Thanks. Haven and Jan helped a ton. And Miah, too, of course." Joanna was careful to include Miah, and the little girl preened with the attention.

Jan turned to Derek from her end of the table. "Derek, I figured you would bring Megan. The two of you really seemed to hit it off the other day!"

With one simple question, it seemed like all eyes were on him. He saw Aiden's surprised expression. "Who's Megan?"

Derek ran a hand over his beard and sighed. "Megan is just a tourist. It's nothing." He looked at Jan, "It's nothing. We had coffee and we went on a hike. Since then, I've barely seen her."

Jan gave him a frown, "Well, that is thoroughly disappointing. You should do something about that."

"A little help here?" he asked Aiden.

Aiden held up his hands, "No way. Better you than me."

The afternoon passed in a blur of laughter and overwhelming amounts of food, like any good Thanksgiving Day should. The only thing Derek regretted was that it was another Thanksgiving Day spent without his mom. Despite his mom's struggles over the past fifteen years, Derek had never given up hope that someday she would be the mother he remembered. Or even a glimmer of that woman. Maybe he could call her and see about Christmas.

Until then, he would do well to remember that family isn't just about who you are related to. His friends had opened their home to him on more than one occasion. Even though his mom didn't live here, Derek had a pretty amazing family in Freedom Ridge.

"HAPPY THANKSGIVING, TRACIE!" Megan said into the phone. Her parents and sister were enjoying the traditional Thanksgiving celebration back in Alabama. Their mouthwatering dinner was surely a far cry from her own. A microwave turkey dinner wasn't exactly her idea of festive, but she was also far too shy to want a pity invitation to a stranger's house for the holiday.

"Megan, oh my goodness! It's so good to hear from you! Are you still holed up in that mountain cabin?"

"Yes, Tracie. Just like I planned."

"I don't know how you do it, being alone so much."

Megan shrugged, "It's what works for me when I'm

writing. Besides, I've made a couple friends," she added defensively.

"I'm glad. When are you coming home?"

"I'll get home on Christmas Eve, I think. Assuming I finish the book."

Megan heard her mother in the background, "Is that Megan?"

"Mom wants to talk with you. But you need to call me next week. I want to hear more about these friends. Are any of them cute?"

Megan rolled her eyes, but she couldn't deny the flash of Derek's face that came to mind. "Hey Mom, Happy Thanksgiving." She heard the clanging of dishes and silverware in the background, and it was hard to hear over the other voices. "I'll let you get back to it. I just called to say hey."

Megan turned back to her solitary dinner and felt more alone after talking to her family. To make up for her lack of Thanksgiving cheer, on Sunday evening she changed out of her typical stretchy pants and put on real jeans to drive to town for the annual Christmas Tree Lighting Ceremony at Town Square. From everything Jan had told her, it was a super sweet community event and while Megan spent her days tangled up in the mess of secrets, action, and intrigue of her novel, she could use some real-world interaction that was a little more heartwarming.

The parking spaces around town square were mostly full and Megan found a spot in a lot down the block. She wrapped her scarf tighter around her neck and tucked her hands into her pockets. The sun was going down, and she admired the twinkling lights hanging from the elm trees along the sidewalk. Most of the shops looked closed, but their autumn-themed window decor had been completely replaced by Christmas lights, bows, and greenery.

As she got closer to the huge tree, she could hear Christmas music playing over a sound system. Families milled about in the park, children tugging on arms as adults tried to talk. There was a line of people waiting at a cute food stand, and she could smell the roasted chestnuts from where she stood.

She felt a bit like a spectator, someone standing on the sidelines of this little town, though she knew from conversation that the event would be attended by locals and tourists alike. A nudge near her kneecap made her look down, and she immediately smiled at the sight of Liberty. She leaned down to pet her, rubbing her hand on Libby's neck and cheek. It was hardly fair to withhold affection from the sweet dog simply because Megan had daydreamed about running her hands through the trimmed beard of Liberty's owner.

The distractingly handsome owner who was, as usual, only steps behind his canine partner, soon stood beside her. Together they faced the large, unlit tree. Megan weighed the uncomfortable silence and resisted the inexplicable urge to lean into the warmth of the muscular man next to her. She cleared her throat. "How was your Thanksgiving?"

"It was good. I went to Joanna's house. Did you meet her at the lodge?"

"I'm not sure, maybe?"

"Jan from Stories and Scones is her mother-in-law."

"Oh, that sounds like fun, then."

"Nicer than alone in a cabin, I'd wager."

She tipped her head in an acknowledgement of the truth. "I'm sure the food was better, anyway."

He smiled. "You don't have to hide away alone on that mountain, Megan."

Shaking her head, she patted his arm. "I know. But I'm leaving in less than a month. It would be foolish to get involved or get too close."

Derek pursed his lips, and she tried not to let her gaze linger there. "I understand. Just," he hesitated, as though unsure of what to say, "if you need anything, let someone know. I worry about you up there all alone."

"You don't need to worry about me. Not too much trouble I can get into while chained to my desk." The expression wasn't too far from the truth, since she was writing and editing for almost six hours a day.

Derek's blue eyes were serious on hers, and Megan felt warm despite the freezing November evening. It was a miracle she could still stand on the icicles that were her legs. Why did people live here? As Derek opened his mouth to respond, a loud voice came over the loud-speaker. Mayor Starling introduced himself and welcomed everyone. He led the countdown, and Megan felt her anticipation kick up as the crowd chanted. "Three...Two...One!"

An icy breath caught in her throat as the lights turned on, and the dark shadow of a towering evergreen tree became a mass of bright colorful lights. It was stunning, and when "Joy to World" started playing, Megan felt the sting of unshed tears. Christmas really was a magical time of year, and Freedom was unlike any place she'd ever spent it. Tonight's festive reminder that Jesus had come to save the world was exactly what she needed.

Liberty stood between Derek and Megan, looking around at the cheering and singing people. Megan studied his profile as Derek admired the tree, wishing once more that she didn't have a huge secret to keep or a hundred reasons to go back to Alabama.

"I'm going to go check out the nativity scene," she said. "Maybe I'll see you around town."

Derek nodded and Megan gave Libby one last neck scratch before walking through the crowd as small children made their way up to the mayor's wife to grab an ornament to hang on the tree. Megan resisted the urge to check behind her to see if Derek was watching her go.

What if he was? Or worse, what if he wasn't and she was the only one feeling the way she did?

DEREK WATCHED MEGAN WALK AWAY. He wasn't sure why she had such an effect on him. At his feet, Liberty let out a whine. "I know, girl. I don't want her to leave either." It didn't seem like he had much choice, though.

He glanced around the square and found the friendly faces of Carson and Nicole standing in line for hot chocolate.

"Hey guys," he said, as he took a place behind them in line. "Welcome back!"

Carson shook his hand and pulled him in for a quick hug. "How are you, man?"

"Same old, same old. How was the honeymoon?"

"Warm," Nicole said with a chuckle. "I forgot how cold it was here!"

Derek laughed, and then Carson looked toward the brightly lit tree and the crowd gathering in front of it to place ornaments. "Quite a turnout this year, isn't it?"

Derek glanced back toward the crowd. Despite the freezing temperatures, the tree lighting was as busy as ever. Maybe more so. Ever since Kevin took over as the manager of the Freedom Ridge Resort, the Resort and its guests had felt a little more like part of the community.

"Always fun to kick off Christmas like this," Derek conceded, nodding toward the waiting cashier. Even if he felt a little Scrooge-y this year, Christmas was special. Maybe he would give his mom a call and invite her to town. If anything could bring their family together, he had to believe it was Christmas magic and a whole lot of prayer. He should really do better about that part.

After they all had the classic hot chocolate, Derek wandered toward the nativity scene, giving Libby a gentle tug on her lead in a mostly unneeded reminder that the live donkeys and sheep were not to play with.

He saw a familiar red coat huddled on the steps of the gazebo and took a seat beside Megan. Her cheeks and nose were the cutest shade of pink and Megan shivered as she rubbed her gloved hands together. "It's cold as a frosted frog out here. And it's only six-thirty, but it feels like midnight between the cold and the dark."

Derek chuckled at her southern twang and handed her the hot chocolate he hadn't tried yet. "Here, I think you need this more than I do."

She took it and held the warm cup to her cheek with a sigh before moving it to her lips and taking a sip. Derek couldn't tear his eyes away from the way her delicate lips blew gently on the opening. He turned away, scolding himself. "How's your project going? You said you're a writer?"

Megan nodded. "It's going alright. That's the thing about writing a book. It's kind of like a rollercoaster where you vacillate between thinking you are a genius and a hack and then back again."

"So are you a genius or a hack today?" he asked with a crooked smile.

"Well, I decided to skip writing and come to this, so I'm going to go with genius."

"What kind of book is it?" Derek hadn't missed that she'd let a little more slip about her *project*.

Megan stared at the disposable cup in her hands as she answered, "Oh, you know. Just a book."

"You're dodging my question." Maybe she was embarrassed that she wrote romance novels. "Is it a romance novel? Fabio and man chest on the cover?"

Megan laughed out loud and he soaked in the happy sound. "No, it is definitely not that kind of romance novel."

"Ah-hah! So it is a romance novel." She didn't respond, but that was okay. At least he had some answers.

Together, they watched as kids placed ornaments on the tree. It always resulted in a hilariously unbalanced tree, with hundreds of ornaments on the lowest branches, and almost none on higher ones, but the tradition was fun. Mayor Starling's wife had established it years ago.

"Megan?"

"Hmm?" She turned toward him and Derek realized just how close they were sitting on the gazebo step. Somehow, they'd inched together and her face was only inches from his own, her skin warm in the glow of the lights decorating the small structure.

Slowly, Derek moved his arm until it rested on her shoulder, then tucked it gently behind her neck. He eased closer, his eyes still on hers. Waiting for permission or denial, though a rejection might kill him at this point. His entire body was on high alert, the same way it was when he was evaluating risk or listening for any sign of a missing person. His gaze dropped to her lips, and he imagined what it would be like to taste her.

Megan's eyes fell closed and Derek's breath caught. He closed his own and started to cross the short gap between their lips. Then, his eyes flew open when he was pushed away from Megan. He found Liberty standing between them, her front paws on the step and her head nudging the arm that was wrapped around the beautiful woman next to him.

Could there be a more inconvenient time for his dog to decide she needed attention? Derek let out a chuckle as the tension of the moment evaporated, like his warm breath into the cold, dry air.

"I should head back," Megan said with a shy smile and a nervous laugh.

"Yeah, okay. Drive safely. Those roads are tricky at night." He thought about all the things that could happen on the way there, then touched her arm. "Will you call me when you get there so I know you're safe?" He spoke the question softly, so only she would hear.

She hesitated for a moment, her brown eyes searching his. Then, she nodded once and stood. For the second time that night, Derek watched her leave and wished he didn't have to. Then, before the cheery Christmas music could grate his nerves too badly, Derek grabbed Libby's lead and headed back to his car.

8

*a*bout two weeks later, Derek stared at his phone as he sat on the steps outside DK9 Security. Bitter wind swirled around him, and the cold of the concrete steps was slowly seeping through his jeans. He looked up to the dark clouds in the west, but he mostly looked past them, hoping for an answer. He had been praying for the last two weeks about reaching out to his mom or dad. Every year around this time, he hemmed and hawed and tried to decide if things would ever be better for them. Or if losing his sister had ripped the family apart completely.

Libby nudged his arm with a soft whine. She was well-tuned to his emotions and usually tried to get close to him when he was agitated. With a deep exhale, he pressed the contact entry for Paula Trine. It still irked him that she had gone back to her maiden name after the divorce.

"Yeah?" The raspy voice that greeted him was familiar but uncomforting.

"Hey, Mom. It's Derek."

"I figured it was you," his mom replied in an uninterested tone.

He stood, needing to pace while they talked. "Well, I just wanted to check in. It's almost Christmas and all."

"So what? What does someone like me want with Christmas anyway?"

"You could be happy, Mom," he said. He had to believe that was true. Joy was beyond circumstance.

Her laughter was dark and cynical, full of venom. "Still a foolish little boy, I see. You'll never save her, Derek. She's gone. No matter how many mutts you train, you'll always be the little boy who lost his sister in the woods." Her anger caught up with her and Paula paused to cough extensively. She wheezed one final cough and then growled. "Stop calling me, boy. At Christmas or any other time."

"You don't mean that--" he protested, but the beep in his ear told him that his mother had hung up. The urge to chuck his phone at the brick wall was strong, but he shoved it in his pocket instead and whistled for Libby as he marched toward the Jeep.

When Derek was angry or frustrated, and his blood boiled with injustice and unforgiveness, he escaped to the one place he knew would provide solace. Six minutes later, Derek threw the Jeep in park on a spur of gravel road and hopped out, grabbing his hat and pulling it over his ears. He let Libby out, but didn't bother clipping on a leash. He didn't want to train. Derek just needed to climb a steep hill and pretend his family hadn't been torn apart twenty years ago.

An inch or two of snow remained in a few places, but

the slightly soft mud dotted the landscape as he trekked through familiar trees. He talked to Libby, who stayed close. He yelled at God, because he knew God could handle his anger. And he hiked. Light snow started to fall, but he barely noticed.

A while later, the snow transitioned to icy sleet and the light began to fade. Amidst the pelting rhythm of ice hitting trees, Derek looked around. He knew where he was. He knew every inch of this mountain by now. But he'd definitely gone farther than he thought. The snow was falling harder now, along with the sleet. This was a hiker's worst nightmare. Checking his watch, Derek saw he'd been hiking for hours, at least six miles from his starting place. In the rapidly accumulating snow and now potential of ice, it would take three times that long to go back.

His hat was soaked with sweat, snow, and a frozen combination of the two. He wiggled his toes. They were stiff and cold. Derek tipped his head back and scolded himself for the amateur mistakes.

Libby whined and nudged his hand. "It's okay, girl. We'll figure this out."

Odds were this was just a normal snow, and it would pass in a few hours. But that would be a long few hours, and he could very well end up with frostbite in the non-winter hiking shoes he wore and without the heavy wool socks he usually wore.

Wind whipped through the trees, and he felt the sting of ice on his nose, though it was mostly numb. No, his best option was to go to the nearest cabin and wait out the storm. Building a mental picture of the mountain in his head, Derek mapped the possible cabins. Megan was only a mile away. It wasn't exactly close when trudging through deepening snow with no light and snow blowing across the ground, but it was his best shot. If he couldn't get there, his next best option was to build an igloo, and well, he'd rather try for the cabin.

"Come on, girl. Let's go find Megan."

It felt like he'd been trudging up the mountain for hours, but Derek's watch kept insisting it had only been forty minutes. Using his phone as a flashlight and the GPS feature on his watch, he crept closer to the location of Megan's cabin. But his feet felt like blocks of ice and each step was harder than the last. When he reached the tree-line and saw the dim glow of lights inside the cabin through the blowing snow, Derek gave a raw shout of joy. Every muscle ached, and he nearly tripped and fell. The snow was up to his knees and without the shield of the trees, the wind cut deeper through his coat and nearly pushed him over.

So close, just a few more steps.

Libby ran ahead and barked at the door, the same insistent bark she gave when alerting him to the source of a scent. "Good girl," he whispered as he collapsed on the step behind her.

9

a persistent noise interrupted the howling of the wind around the cabin and Megan tilted her head to listen for it again. She frowned, then jogged down the stairs of the loft. A glance out the picture window revealed nothing but blowing snow highlighted in the exterior lights. The sound continued--short, sharp… barks?

Megan opened the front door, flinching at the wave of wind and snow that assaulted her. "Libby?"

Libby whined before turning back and taking a few steps down the porch. She sat and barked again.

Megan gasped. "Derek!" Despite her lack of shoes or coat, Megan stepped into the foot of snow and grabbed Derek's arm, trying to tug him inside. He didn't budge, and her toes were freezing. She repositioned herself and wrapped her elbows under his shoulders before counting to three and pulling with all her strength.

She landed in a heap on the welcome mat just inside

the front door, Derek's head in her lap. He looked peaceful, though his nose was an angry red color. She pulled him in further and shut the door, closing out the howling wind and frigid temperature.

Her eyes darted around the cabin, unsure of what to do next. The fireplace in the living room. "Please, let him be okay!" she pleaded with God as she pulled off Derek's stocking cap. Then, she dragged him across the wood floor to the rug in front of the fireplace. She praised God that she had started a fire earlier. Megan pulled off his boots and socks, and flinched at the icy, damp skin of his feet. How long had he been out in this storm? Was he searching for someone?

As she gave him a once-over, Megan realized all of his clothes were likely soaked. But trying to get his coat off with Derek still passed out seemed daunting. Then, a low moan emerged from his throat and Megan moved from her position near his waste to cradle his cheek in her hand. "Derek, Derek. Wake up. Come on…"

His eyes fluttered open, and Megan rejoiced at the sight of his baby blue eyes, though they remained unfocused. He groaned again and tried to sit up, but Megan pushed him back down. "It's okay, you're okay. You made it to my cabin. Just take a second. Then we'll sit you up and take off these wet clothes, okay?"

Derek nodded and shut his eyes again. Megan pulled a log from the small stack and added it to the fire before returning to his side. "Okay, Derek are you ready? I'm going to help you sit up."

Once he was sitting, Megan unzipped his coat with

---

trembling fingers. Ice flaked off the zipper as she tugged it down. She gingerly flipped the coat open and helped Derek get his frozen arms out. When she saw what he wore under the coat, Megan gasped. Just a button-down shirt with his company logo on it. He was nowhere near dressed for hiking in the cold weather, let alone the blizzard that had surprised everyone in town with the speed with which it arrived.

"Oh my word, Derek. You could have died out there." She unbuttoned the shirt and tugged it off, leaving him in an undershirt.

"So c-c-cold," he chattered. Megan nudged him closer to the fireplace and grabbed a large blanket from the couch.

"I know, it's going to be okay. We'll get you warmed up." She glanced at his jeans. "Derek, I'm going to need you to take off all your clothes so you can get dry and warm. Can you do that or do you need help." A blush rose on her cheeks, despite her attempt to stay practical.

He shook his head and grunted. "I got it." She turned around to give him privacy and jumped when his wet jeans and undershirt landed in a pile near her feet. "Alright, I'm done."

When she turned around, Derek was seated in front of the fire, covered from the shoulders down with the quilt. Libby curled up next to him, her head on his knee. Megan grabbed the pile of wet clothes and hung them in the bathroom. Then, she went to the kitchen to get water for her two unexpected houseguests.

She brought the lukewarm water to them and sat close, absorbing the silence and watching Derek stare blankly into the fire. Outside, the wind still howled angrily around the cabin. From what Megan had seen online earlier, the storm was a big one. She had planned to hunker down for a few days, but she wasn't too worried. Until she heard the barking.

Megan couldn't fathom what Derek had been doing out in the blizzard. It seemed so unlike the prepared boy scout who had taken her on a hike in October. He'd been ready for anything that day. Not today, though.

"How are you feeling?" she asked quietly, not wanting to startle him.

"Foolish, mostly. But at least I'm alive," he said.

"What were you doing out in this storm?"

He shook his head. "Lost track of time. I didn't even know there was a storm coming."

She nodded. "Weather channel said it came up fast, and started dumping snow and ice before the predictions even started."

"Sorry to intrude, I guess."

Megan scoffed, "Intrude? I thought you were dead on my porch, Derek! You scared me half to death. I'm just glad you made it here and that Libby was able to get my attention." She shuddered. "I could have walked out in three days and found you frozen to the front step."

"Good girl, Libby," he said, rubbing the dog's ears. "Well, I'll get out of your hair as soon as I'm warmed up a bit.

Megan drew back. "You're crazy as a betsy bug if you think you're going anywhere. The roads are covered in an inch of ice and eight inches of snow and it's still coming down. The wind is blowing so hard you can't see a foot in front of your face. I can't believe you even found my cabin in this storm, but now that you're here, you aren't going anywhere." She couldn't believe she was the one who had to tell him this. Surely he knew better. Maybe the blizzard had frozen some of his brain cells.

Despite her emphatic speech, Derek sat motionless in front of the fireplace, his eyes focused someplace within or beyond the fire.

"Derek?"

At the sound of his name, he finally turned his head toward her. "Sorry, yeah. I guess I'll stay. Can I see the weather when you get a chance?"

"Drink your water, and I'll go get my computer." She intentionally waited until he took a drink from the tepid mug before retrieving her laptop from the loft. She pulled up the weather website and showed him the radar map, a mess of light blue, pink, and purple.

He frowned at the image and looked around the cabin. "Boy, am I glad to be in here."

"How are your feet?"

"They hurt, but that's actually a good sign." He wiggled his toes and pulled in one leg to examine his toes. "Just a bit of frostnip, which is downright miraculous with my stupidity today. Do you have any painkillers?"

Megan got some from the bathroom and handed them to him, grateful he seemed okay. The blanket slipped as he grabbed the pills from her hand, revealing his bare shoulder and arm. "Umm, I'll see if I can find you something to wear." Megan knew even as she walked back to the bedroom that finding something in her closet that would fit the muscular man currently naked in her living room was unlikely.

She rummaged through her drawers and found an XL T-shirt she usually wore to bed. It was hot pink and had Panama City Beach splashed across it in lime green. As for pants? Her own yoga pants and jeans were out of the question. She found a ratty pair of baggy sweat pants. She normally rolled the waist up 3-4 times and they still dwarfed her small frame, so hopefully that would give him a little something to work with until his clothes were dry.

She carried the clothes back to him and gave an apologetic smile. "I think this is the best I can do."

He raised his eyebrow and then chuckled at the t-shirt. "Pink's not really my color." Then his eyes went solemn, "Seriously, Megan, thank you. For everything." The way his low voice hummed her name had her ears burning, and she nodded, since all her words seemed to be caught somewhere between her stomach and her throat.

"I'll let you get dressed whenever you think you're ready, then I can heat up some soup or something? Or soup first, then clothes?" Megan took a deep breath to cut off her nervous rambling. "Sorry. I've just never dealt with anything like this."

"You're doing amazing. I'll get dressed and then maybe soup here by the fire?" Megan nodded and busied herself in the kitchen while Derek started shrugging on the pink T-shirt. Somehow, he was going to put on the sweatpants and she didn't need to be watching.

A couple minutes later, with help from the microwave, Megan brought a warm bowl of soup for Derek and a few slices of lunchmeat on a plate for Liberty. It wasn't exactly gourmet dog food, but Libby devoured the meat and then licked the plate before turning her gorgeous brown eyes up to Megan as if to ask, "Is that it?"

Derek patted her head and laughed. "That's enough for now, Libby. We'll have some more in a bit, after your stomach has settled." He spooned the soup and gave a satisfied sigh. Megan clicked through the forecast on her computer and tried not to hover.

After he'd finished the soup, Derek hobbled over to the kitchen and put his empty bowl near the sink. The sweat pants ended just above his ankles and hugged his thighs far tighter than her own, and she bit back a giggle. Then, instead of returning to his spot on the rug, Derek grabbed his blanket and reclined on the couch. Almost immediately, his eyes were closed and his breathing was deep and even. Libby paced for a moment, then spun a few circles and laid down on the floor near his shoulders, closing her own eyes.

After she turned off the overhead lights and stoked the fire, Megan pulled a small afghan over her own legs and curled up in the armchair. Her laptop sat on the coffee table a few feet away, but work seemed out of reach. Instead, she grabbed a book and started reading. Before long, she too was rubbing her eyes and snuggling deeper into the chair to steal some shuteye.

When Megan opened her eyes, the first things she noticed was the darkness of the room and the continued howl of wind. The second thing she noticed was the soft snoring of someone across the room. Whether it was Derek or Liberty, she couldn't tell. The fire was smoldering, muted red coals emitting the only light in the room. Wait, hadn't she left the lamp on?

She jumped up, her afghan falling to the floor. After glancing at the microwave clock, Megan tried the light switch to confirm her suspensions. The power was out.

10

---

*D*erek woke to wet sandpaper rubbing against his hand, and he pulled away from the contact, wrapping the blanket tighter around himself. It was chilly in his room. His eyes flew open, and he stared at the unfamiliar vaulted ceiling, which looked grey and muted in the early morning light. Memories of the night before flooded him. He was at Megan's cabin. He had nearly died because of his reckless impulse to trek through the woods.

A quick glance at his watch told him it was nearly eight in the morning. Why was it so cold though? He sat up and found Megan at the kitchen table, huddled in a blanket. The only light he could see streamed through the mostly iced windows.

"Ummm, good morning?"

"The power is out," Megan responded.

He winced. That's not great. Better than freezing to death in the snow last night, but still not great.

"Okay. Well, let's get this fire going." At least they would have some localized heat from that.

"I put the last log on it last night when I woke up. I think there is more by the shed, but I'm not really sure. I haven't used the fire much to be honest."

Derek rubbed his hands over his face and tried to press the drowsiness away. He was pretty sure he hadn't moved a muscle all night after falling asleep on that couch. A million words in the English language and not a single combination of them could adequately explain how exhausted he felt.

Libby laid her head in his lap, and he rubbed her ears. She needed to go outside, but what was the storm like now? Derek pushed himself up to standing and shuffled over to the door. He opened it a crack and peeked out. The snow was about two feet high at the door, and he couldn't even see Megan's car parked in the driveway thirty feet away. The wind was still blowing everything. He swallowed the bad word that wanted to escape and looked down at Libby's hopeful face and wagging tail. "Give me a minute, girl," he said, shutting the door.

He rummaged in the kitchen cabinets until he found a large mixing bowl, then returned to the door and began to scoop snow from the opening, keeping his feet inside. Libby wouldn't go far, but at least this way she could make it a couple feet from the door.

When he stepped aside, Libby went out and returned a few seconds later with snow clinging to her coat. They needed to find a shovel. Pete wasn't an amateur, there had to be one in the house somewhere.

"Coat closet?"

Megan pointed to a door near the dining table. Inside, Derek found a snow shovel and a basket with hats, gloves, and scarves. "Bless you, Petey!"

He still had no shoes, but he got a pair of socks from Megan and opened the kitchen door again. Derek cleared a path to the steps, carefully stepping where he'd already shoveled. Thankfully, the snow was only that deep near the door because of a drift. Closer to the steps, there was less snow, but a thick layer of ice had him slipping and nearly falling into the walls of the snow ditch he'd cleared. The roads would be nasty.

He went back inside and sent Libby out to try again. She made it farther and took care of business before running back inside. "Good girl!" he clucked his tongue to replicate the training clicker.

Turning to Megan, he sighed. "We'll need firewood at some point, but I'm hoping the wind will die down before we have to go that far. You okay for now?"

Megan pulled the blanket tighter. "Yep. I checked the water heater. It's gas. Want something to eat?"

He collapsed into a chair at the table, already feeling like he needed a nap. Megan set a bowl of cereal and a banana in front of him. His stomach rumbled in appreciation. He gave her a grateful look. "Thank you." She sat, and he looked again at the beautiful woman sitting across from him. "Do you mind if I pray?"

Her eyes widened, and she shook her head. He extended a hand to hers, and when she placed her hand in his, he squeezed it gently.

Derek lowered his eyes and prayed. "Father, I'm so grateful today to be alive and here, with Megan. I know it was only your providence that protected me in the storm and led me to this cabin. Please continue to keep us safe here and everyone else affected by this storm. Please grant us a break in the wind so we can safely get firewood and bless this food to our bodies. In Jesus' name, Amen."

Megan's small voice echoed his own, and their hands parted. Immediately, he missed the contact, but he directed his attention to his plate and devoured his food. Coffee sounded amazing, but that whole electricity thing definitely put a wrinkle in that plan.

"Other than praying for a break in the wind, what is on your agenda today?" He was curious how Megan spent her days, holed up in the cabin alone. It seems like it would get old quickly without even a dog for company. Maybe he could let her borrow one until she left.

"I don't know. I need to spend some time with my book. I'm struggling with a storyline, and need to flesh it out. Other than that? I guess I'll hang out with you."

"What's so hard about two people meet and fall in love? I thought romances were simple. It's not like you are writing a Marcus Warner book with four storylines that somehow intertwine later in the book."

Megan pushed her food around on her plate and he kicked himself. "I'm sorry, I didn't mean that what you do isn't difficult. I can't handle writing a website, let alone a whole book. I just meant--"

"It's fine. You're right. I'm probably overthinking it." Her voice was clipped, and she got up from the table, despite her plate still half full. "I'm going to take a shower and try to write a bit." With that, Megan disappeared down the hallway, leaving him and Libby alone. That could have gone better.

MEGAN SHUT herself in the bedroom and paced. Last night, she'd been so concerned about making sure Derek was alright that she didn't even consider the ramifications of being trapped with him for several days. She was a terrible liar. At home, she mostly avoided in-depth conversations with anyone who wasn't already in her inner circle. That is, her family and her best friend, Elizabeth.

Everyone else was a risk she couldn't take. And that included Derek. So what should she do until the storm passed and the road was clear? She couldn't let Derek figure out that she was Marcus Warner. All it would take was one passing mention for her name and location to end up on social media and for Tristan to find her.

Still, she didn't want to lie. As she finished her shower, she resolved to tell the truth. But if Derek happened to make assumptions that she didn't correct? Well, that was for the best.

When Megan went out to the living room, Derek was pulling on socks and his hiking shoes. He glanced up at her before tying the laces. "I'm going to go track down some wood. It's only going to get colder in here as the day goes on."

"Are you sure it's okay out there?" The idea of him trekking all the way to the shed in the blowing snow made her nervous.

He just nodded. "I'll be alright. But, since I can't see much out there, we're going to make a rope I can use to find my way back." He looked around, "Any ideas for what we can use as rope?"

While Derek debated between cutting up sheets or cutting up towels, Megan dug through the utility closet and came up with two long extension cords. She brought them out, one in each arm and heavier than she imagined, Derek looked at her with surprise.

"That's perfect."

Megan watched with trepidation as he donned two hats, wrapped a scarf all the way around his face leaving a slit for his eyes, and pulled on two pairs of gloves.

"You look like Ralphie's little brother," she said with a smile, referencing her favorite Christmas movie.

Derek laughed, the sound muffled by the scarf. He raised his arms to shoulder height. "I can't put down my arms!" He mimicked the iconic scene, and Megan doubled over with laughter.

"For real, be careful," she reminded him when the laughter had subsided.

Megan stepped close and tucked the end of the scarf into the collar of his coat so it wouldn't come undone. She looked up to meet his eyes. He was stone still, and she opened her mouth to speak, but nothing came out. There was more to say, but she didn't know what or how to say it. She closed her mouth and patted his chest. "Be safe," she whispered.

With a deep breath and a nod, Derek moved toward the door, grabbing the extension cords. As Megan watched through the window, he tied a cord to the porch column and then unwound it as he went down the steps. The snow was up to his knees and still blowing like crazy. Before long, she couldn't see him anymore.

Megan chewed the ragged edge of a fingernail and waited. How long would it take? How long could he be out there and be okay? A shadowy form came closer, and she could make out the outline of Derek carrying a stack of wood in one arm, tracing the extension cord with another. Libby barked at the thudding noise when Derek dropped the wood by the door. Then, he turned around, retreating back into the snow.

Megan put on her coat and hat then moved to the door. She brought the wood inside before closing it again and leaning against it. A few minutes later, a loud thud behind her let her know that Derek had brought another armful.

For thirty minutes, they continued. By the time Derek stepped in the door, snow was clinging to the scarf and stocking hat. He closed the door and leaned against it, dropping the final load of firewood inside the door. Megan had carried some to the living room, but most of it was still haphazardly strewn near the entrance of the kitchen in her hustle to get it inside.

As Derek pulled off the snow-and-ice-crusted winter gear, Megan carried small stacks of wood and added it to the pile by the fireplace. Derek sat at the table to pull off wet socks, then wiggled out of stiff, icy jeans to reveal her sweatpants underneath. Then he crossed the room, tugged on the armchair to pull it near the fire, then huddled in it with blankets. Not a word had been said since he got back inside.

"You okay?" Megan brushed the hair from his forehead as she stood next to the chair. His eyes were already closed, and he nuzzled against her hand with a murmur before falling asleep. Megan grabbed the wet socks and jeans where he'd left them and hung them up to dry. Hopefully Derek didn't routinely leave his laundry lying about and this was a special circumstance. Either way, she'd give him grace this time.

It was hard not to admire a man who had trudged back and forth in a blizzard to get firewood for her. If he hadn't been here, she would have just suffered the cold temperatures in the cabin for however many days.

She was very glad Derek was here. Giving his sleeping form one last glance, she felt her resolve crack, just a bit. Like thawing ice in the early spring. Maybe trusting someone would be worth it. Maybe trusting Derek would be worth it.

11

*D*erek woke with a start, his body warm and stiff. He shrugged off one of the blankets and looked around for Megan. He didn't see her anywhere, so he added a log to the fire that was slowly dying and looked at his watch. The firewood journey had taken most of the morning and his much-needed nap had taken the rest.

Derek peered through the door of the bedroom and found Megan asleep in her bed, huddled under the covers. Back here, away from the fire, the temperature of the cabin had already dropped well into the fifties. If the power didn't come back on, they would need to sleep near the fire tonight.

He tiptoed quietly through the cabin, stopping to clean up in the bathroom and brush his teeth with a finger and some toothpaste. He glanced at the kitchen then up the stairs to the loft. Unable to quell his curiosity, he took the stairs. In the loft, he found a tidy desk and a laptop. A single notebook and pen sitting next to it.

Fingering the notebook, the urge to open it was overwhelming. The sound of a door closing below had him freezing in place before hurrying back down the steps and into the kitchen. When Megan appeared around the corner, running her fingers through her hair, he tried to act casual as he rummaged through the cupboards, despite his still-racing heart.

"Hungry?" he held up a jar of peanut butter.

"No bread," she said with a shrug.

Derek scratched his beard. "Crackers?" she shook her head. "Apples?"

"A-ha. Yes, apples."

Derek made a passable lunch with apple slices dipped in peanut butter, along with some chips and milk. "We'll have to figure out what we can cook for dinner. Do you have any aluminum foil?"

Megan frowned. "I think so? But the oven doesn't work."

"How about this? We will have a competition. Whoever makes the best meal from whatever we can find in the kitchen wins. You cook tonight, and I'll cook tomorrow."

"Okay… but I get to choose my ingredients tonight so you don't take all the good ones."

"Deal." Derek smiled. Years of cooking campfire dinners had prepared him for this moment.

The phone on the wall rang, and they both jumped at the unexpected sound. Derek's eyes got wide. How had he forgotten that the cabin had a landline? And one with an old-fashioned cord and everything. He raced to the phone. "Hello?"

Pete's familiar voice came through the speaker. "Derek, is that you?"

"Yeah, it's me."

"Oh, thank God you're okay. A snowplow reported your Jeep off the highway when the storm was just picking up. We thought you were stuck out there. How'd you end up with Megan?"

Derek just shook his head. "Long story that starts with me being an idiot. But we're fine. Power is out up here, though. What's it like in town?"

Pete clucked his tongue. "It's nasty, man. Power is out here, too. And the roads are a sheet of ice under the snow. They plowed some of it, but that was worse. And it's still blowing around like crazy. I talked to Starling this morning, and he said he thought the town might start clearing out tomorrow, but I bet it'll be two days after that before they clear all the way up to the cabin."

"Well, don't worry about us. We've got firewood and water. Whenever someone can get a truck up here, I'd appreciate it. Any chance you know where Jared is? I left him with the dogs yesterday afternoon before the storm hit."

"I'm betting he stayed there, but I'll see if I can get him. My cellphone is still working in town, maybe his is, too.

"Thanks, Pete. I owe you one."

"Be safe. Stay warm."

"You too."

He hung up the phone and sagged against the wall. He hadn't realized how worried he was about his dogs, or the people in town. He'd never considered that people in town would be worried about him. He was the searcher, not the lost.

Pete would be able to spread the word that he was okay. And someone would manage to take care of the dogs. Freedom was a community that way. In hard times, people stepped up to care for each other. That was one reason he had chosen Freedom for his home base. It was a great place to train dogs, but it wasn't far from where his sister had gone missing. His job with the dogs and his expertise on search and rescue meant he had the chance to prevent the same thing from happening again.

"Everything okay?" Megan asked. She stood a few feet away from him and the phone, waiting while he had finished the call.

"Yeah. That was Pete, just checking on you, I guess. He was surprised to find me here, though."

"So was I," she chuckled.

"Honestly, I'm not sure there is any place I would rather be." He stepped close and tucked his hand under her ear. A stroke of his thumb revealed her skin was as soft as he'd imagined. He swallowed. "I haven't stopped thinking about you since we met in the woods two months ago."

"Me either," she whispered. That was all the invitation he needed, and Derek bent down slowly, pulling her close and shrinking the distance between them.

"If you don't want me to kiss you, now is your chance to say so."

In response, Megan's hands gripped the hot pink t-shirt he wore and pulled him into the kiss he'd been antic-ipating for so long. Her warm, soft lips played against his, and he turned slightly so she was pressed against the kitchen counter, placing one hand on her waist. He drank her in, every contour of her lips under his and every curve of her neck under his fingers. Her small, soft body was heaven against his. "You're perfect," he whispered before capturing her lips again.

Derek had never experienced a kiss like this. It was all-consuming, and if the blizzard raging outside had torn the roof off the cabin, he might not have noticed. When they finally broke the kiss, Derek couldn't have said if it was one minute later or ten. He stepped back to create space between them, though his fingers itched to tangle in her hair and finger with the hem of her shirt again.

He said a quick prayer for self-control and ran a hand over his beard. Megan blew out a shaky breath. "I, uh... I've never done that before," she said. Derek quirked an eyebrow at her.

"What do you mean?"

"No one has ever..."

"Kissed you?" He had a hard time believing that. Megan was sexy and funny. Plus, her southern accent would very likely have him trying to grant her every wish.

"Not like that," she said with the slightest hint of awe in her voice.

Derek felt the surge of pride and a hint of smug satisfaction at her response. He'd be more than happy to do it again, but a twinge of conviction told him they both needed to cool off.

"That was definitely the best kiss I've ever had," he replied, reaching for her hand.

"No one ever wanted to kiss me," she said, staring at their linked fingers.

"Trust me, Meg. That's their loss." To prove his point, Derek stepped forward and pressed his lips against hers again. Lighter this time, it was a kiss that soothed the ache of longing left by the intensity of the first.

He squeezed her hand and let go. "I'm going to go stoke the fire. The one in the living room, that is," he said with a wink.

MEGAN BLUSHED AND TURNED AWAY, busying herself returning the kitchen to its normal orderly state. The lingering effects of that kiss on her brain made it slightly hard to function. Her thoughts were centered on how fantastic it felt to be held and kissed and desired like that. She swore she could still feel the soft hair of his beard and the heat of his mouth as he pulled her close and drove every thought or objection from her mind.

Surely she should object, right? It was definitely not prudent to get involved in a vacation fling. Even if the man in question was handsome and strong and charming and had the cutest dogs she had ever met. Megan had survived by making smart choices, thinking things through and analyzing them from every possible angle. And no matter how long she analyzed this, it wasn't going to become the smart decision. The wise thing to do would be finish her book and go back to Alabama.

But, as she absently wiped the counter and shivered in the cold kitchen, her gaze slid back across the open-concept room to Derek. He finished stacking more logs on the fire and obliged when Libby rolled onto her back begging for a belly rub. The snow out the window, the fire, the dog, and yes, the man, all created a picture-perfect scene she wished were hers for more than today or more than this storm.

Megan forced herself to turn away from the cozy scene on the fireplace rug and rummaged through cabinets to plan her meal. She had watched every season of Chopped on the Food Network and was more than confident that she could figure out a way to fix something for dinner with no microwave. Or stove. Or oven.

Maybe this would be harder than she thought. Pasta was out, so was eggs or anything with meat she had to cook. Unless she could figure out a way to cook on the fire.

She went back to the fridge and glanced in the meat drawer. Ah-ha! Hot dogs. She could do a classic campfire theme tonight. Hotdogs roasted on the fire, and she even had marshmallows, though no graham crackers. She considered the Chopped contestants and went back to the cupboard. A yellow package of fudge striped cookies beckoned her from the back shelf. Purchased on a whim, they would be a perfect substitute for traditional s'more ingredients.

Dinner might not be amazing, but the theme and taste should earn her some points. Satisfied with her plan, she went back toward the living room and found Derek once again asleep on the small sofa.

Despite the temptation to take a nap of her own, Megan knew she needed to work. She only had another ten days before she planned to leave town. Her rough draft was finished but something was missing. While Derek slept, Megan dove into her story and edited. An hour or two later, she startled at the sight of someone in her peripheral vision. Derek leaned nonchalantly against the wall near the stairs. She clapped a hand to her racing heart and gave a nervous laugh. "You scared me."

She hurriedly saved and closed her laptop and notebook. The last thing she needed was Derek seeing Jett's name on the screen.

"What are you working on?" Though his tone was merely curious, Megan felt her pulse accelerate.

"I'm editing. Deadline is just a few weeks away, but I'm trying to be done before I leave for Christmas with my family. My laptop had a couple hours of battery at least."

"Where is your family?"

Megan stood and started headed downstairs, thankful when he followed her. "Birmingham, mostly. Some in Tuscaloosa." They reached the bottom steps and she returned the question. "How about yours?"

Derek's eyes fluttered closed and he shook his head. "Don't really have much family anymore. My parents split up, and my mom haunts the lowbrow casinos in Vegas. Dad died a few years back driving drunk." He stared toward the living room. "After my sister, Lyndsey, went missing when she was twelve, neither of them could handle each other. Or me," he added. Megan's heart broke at sadness in his voice. "I was sixteen. I should have been watching out for her." Anguish caused his voice to crack and turn to a hoarse whisper. "Every now and then, I wonder if..." Derek shook his head again and gave her a tight smile. He swallowed and started again, "It doesn't matter. What happened is what happened, and it's too late to change it. I just try my best to make sure it doesn't happen to another family."

Megan stepped in, overwhelmed by the urge to comfort him and tucked her head against his chest. His arms encircled her, and they stood at the base of the stairs in silence for a moment. She squeezed tightly, as if she could convey with an embrace all the words that wouldn't come. What could she say? She couldn't understand the loss of a sibling. Her own sister was her best friend. She couldn't understand the hurt of having your parents fall apart and turn their back on you. Her own parents were her biggest supporters and strongest example of faith. All Megan could do was hold him and hope he understood that she cared.

12

——————

*A*s the light outside faded late in the afternoon, the temperature in every part of the house except the living room dropped further and further. The fire was warm, but it could only radiate so far.

When Megan pulled out hotdogs and metal coat hangers to roast them on, Derek couldn't help but smile. She could have gone with cold ham and cheese sandwiches, but with the first bite of smoky, charred hotdog, he realized how welcome the warm food was in his belly. Libby appreciated the hotdogs he gave her as well.

"Wait, wait, wait," Megan added with glee. "We haven't even made it to the pièce de résistance." Her southern accent imitating the French pronunciation was the best thing he'd heard all year, and he started laughing. His eyes were closed, and he felt something bounce off his cheek and land in his lap. He looked down to see a marshmallow.

"S'mores?" he asked, excitedly. "I haven't had a s'more in years."

"Mmm-hmmm," Megan confirmed. "Well, kind of." She pulled out a package and handed him a napkin with two fudge striped cookies. "This is Chopped, after all. We are being creative."

"Works for me." He skewered two marshmallows on the end of his coat hanger and poked it into the fire, letting them catch fire before pulling them back out and extinguishing it.

He wiggled his eyebrows when he caught Megan watching in horror. "You can't ruin a marshmallow like that!" Her eyes sparkled in the glow of the fire and Derek wanted to kiss her shocked little mouth closed.

Instead he placed his blackened marshmallows between the cookies and took a bite. The marshmallow was mostly unwarmed on the inside and the slight ashy taste of the burned outside was comfortingly familiar. He could almost believe he was on a camping trip instead of stranded in a blizzard.

He watched, amused, as Megan made her way to the edge of the fireplace and tucked her marshmallows into an empty spot, away from the higher flames. She slowly rotated the hanger with precise uniform movements. Derek admired her patience as he finished his s'more and skewered two more marshmallows. He'd be six cookies in before she got to eat one. Finally, as Derek assembled his second s'more, Megan removed her golden brown marshmallow from the fire, examined it closely, and gingerly set it on her cookie.

He watched, mesmerized, as she took a bite. Marshmallow oozed out from between her cookies and stuck to the corner of her lip. When she gave a satisfied moan,

Derek felt his resolve crumble. Megan finished her treat and wiped her hands on a napkin, then her lips.

"Aren't you going to eat that?" Megan's question interrupted his staring. He glanced down at his s'more.

"I think maybe I need the chef-prepared version to fairly judge your competition entry."

Megan rolled her eyes. "You just want me to roast you a proper marshmallow."

"Well, yeah." He ate the second ashy dessert while waiting for her to methodically roast him two new marshmallows.

"You're going to get sick," she commented while handing him the completed s'more.

"Nah. Besides, I almost died last night. I deserve this."

He had to admit, the melty, gooey, marshmallow was better. But slower. He was often impatient. Jared usually reminded him to be patient with the training regimen, but other than with the dogs, Derek wanted to move fast.

He finished his dessert, and they cleaned up the packaging while Libby sniffed the carpet for crumbs. After he cleared the porch walk and let the dog out for one last bathroom break, they settled back in front of the fire. Derek happily opened his arms to wrap Megan in them as he leaned against the armchair and she spread the blanket over both of them.

They watched the fire crackle and Derek told her stories about some of his most memorable search and rescue missions. Like the time he found a woman twelve feet up in a tree who refused to come down. He ran his fingers through Megan's hair and relished in the feel of her nestled in his arms. Slowly, she turned her face to his, wordlessly searching for something. And Derek knew exactly what to give her. He captured her mouth with his and the long, sweet goodnight kiss was perfect and unhurried.

Maybe slow had its merits.

Reluctantly, Derek ended the kiss. It was getting late and sleep beckoned. Megan retrieved the comforter and extra blankets from the bedroom and they made up separate pallets on the floor in front of the fire and laid down. Libby curled up between them, a canine chaperone.

Derek stared up at the shadows of the vaulted ceiling, his hands under his head and elbows wide. He could feel Megan just across the room, her slow breathing was comforting. She was steady and methodical and organized. And while most wouldn't classify Derek as reckless or haphazard, he was well aware of his tendency for impulsive decisions. Like the hike in the woods, or the kiss against the kitchen cabinets, even the memory of which kicked his pulse up a notch.

There was something soothing about being here in this cabin with her. He'd meant what he said earlier. There was nowhere else he'd rather be. He was still curious about her writing, and she remained awfully tightlipped about it. Derek couldn't tell if she'd been nervous when he came upstairs, or just surprised to see him. Was she actively trying to keep the details of her work a secret from him, or was Megan always quiet about that part of her life?

He was drawn to her like he had never been to anyone, and that was a bit scary for him. He needed to follow his gut and dig a little deeper before he would let himself fall any further. Derek's instincts and refusal to give up had led him to finding dozens of lost hikers over the years. It culminated in his building the most reputable SAR dog training company in the United States. Before he could consider something more with Megan, Derek needed all the information, especially if there was something she was hiding.

MEGAN ROLLED OVER AND STRETCHED, her fingers skimming the chilly floor. She sat up and saw the fire had dwindled overnight to an ashy pile of coals. Wrapping her sweater tighter around her shoulders, she scooted forward and added a couple of logs, stirring the coals to help them catch. Libby was curled up next to Derek and his hand rested on the dog's back, his blanket partially covering her.

The sky was light, though the house was still cast in the early morning shadow of the mountain. Megan realized why the scene outside was so surprising. She could see the trees in the distance, which for two days had been obscured by violently blowing snow.

The storm had finally passed. She could see the limbs of trees, laden with thick shells of ice and saw dozens within her view had collapsed under the added weight. This storm had left its mark on the forest. Another look at the peaceful form of Derek Held and her heart grew. Perhaps this storm had left its mark on her also.

With a yawn and another stretch, Megan stood and made her way to the kitchen. A quick flick of a lightswitch confirmed what the frigid air told her--the power was still out. She looked longingly at the coffee maker and grabbed a drink of water instead. Thank God Pete had a small generator on the well-pump. He should really consider a generator for the whole house. As much as she enjoyed sleeping feet away from Derek, this whole stranded on a mountain thing would be much more enjoyable with electricity. And heat. And coffee.

Derek barely stirred as Liberty stood and stretched with her paws out long in front of her. She walked over to Megan, tail wagging and pushed her nose into Megan's legs, looking for attention. Megan was happy to oblige and rubbed the dog's ears. She let Liberty outside, who was thrilled to find that the piercing wind had died down, and leapt around in the snow, biting and chasing the pieces she kicked up.

Megan watched through the window at the dog's antics and hummed in appreciation when Derek stepped up behind her and wrapped an arm around her waist. She leaned back against him. "Good morning, beautiful."

The low timbre of his voice did fluttery things to her stomach, and she reveled in the affection. "Good morning. The storm passed in the night."

"Praise God," he replied, and she heard the sincerity in his voice.

Knowing that he also shared the faith that was so important to her was a special gift. If she'd been stranded here with a stranger, who knows what could have happened. Or maybe that was just her writer's imagination running away again. What were the odds that she would run into Derek repeatedly in the woods and in town, and that he would find himself on her doorstep in the middle of a storm?

It felt like God was doing something here, and she was going to roll with it. Libby came back to the door, ready to come in, and Derek pulled away. Megan missed his warmth immediately. While Derek got water and leftover hotdogs for Libby for breakfast, Megan sat back in front of the fire.

Breakfast was granola bars and fruit, and by noon, they were twiddling their thumbs. Megan's laptop battery was finally dead, and while Derek had trekked back to the shed to bring in more wood, it hadn't taken nearly as long. He'd also managed to find a snow shovel in the shed and clear the porch and a path. He'd been outside for over an hour, working up a sweat, despite the still-frigid air.

Lunch was peanut butter and jelly, and then Derek took a nap while Megan read a book. When he woke up, they decided to play a game. The cabin had a few board games, mostly for kids. He left the choice up to her and Scrabble won over Monopoly.

"That's probably better for our relationship. I've heard of families feuding over Monopoly," he joked.

"Yikes. I just figured that I should be able to beat you at Scrabble. I am an author after all."

Derek pretended to be offended, and she kissed the frown off his face. Then, he brightened. "That's okay. Even if you win at Scrabble, I get the chance to be declared Chopped Champion when I fix dinner tonight. Prepare to be amazed."

"Can you actually cook?" Megan asked as she set up

the game board. "I mean, like at home with a stove and all that."

Derek wiggled his eyebrows. "I'll let you be the judge of that. How about you, do you cook?"

She shook her head. "Not really. A few of the basics, but since I live with my sister, we mostly order out or do frozen pizza and the like."

"Oh? Tell me about your sister." Derek's blue eyes looked at her expectantly.

With a shake of her head, Megan smiled. "Tracie is... spirited. She and I couldn't be more different, honestly. She's incredibly disorganized and slightly scatterbrained. But I love her to pieces."

"Younger?"

"How'd you know?" Megan laughed. "Yeah, she's three years younger than me. She's an artist, and one of the bedrooms in our apartment is a studio where she holes up and works on all kinds of things."

"It's cool that you guys are so close."

Megan could hear the hint of sadness in his voice and she asked, "What about you? Do you have roommates or anything?"

He shook his head. "Just Libby. I've got some great friends. Jared works with me at DK9, and Max is a police officer. My buddy Aiden got married last year, and Carson got married a few weeks ago--at that wedding you wouldn't come to," he said with a raised eyebrow. She blushed and covered her face.

"I'm sorry! I didn't think it was a good idea." Her smile disappeared, and she looked up at him. "I'm still not really sure it is, but here we are, so..."

Derek grabbed her hand. "We'll just see where it goes, okay?"

Megan swallowed and nodded. "Yeah, okay."

They played Scrabble and Megan unashamedly whooped him, winning by over two hundred points. He raised his hands in surrender. "No more, I give up." Then, he mockingly bowed down to her. "I declare you Scrabble Master." Then, he stood up and stretched. "I think it's time I go redeem myself by cooking you the best dinner you've ever had that didn't involve a stove."

Megan raised an eyebrow, skeptical of his boastful talk. Figuring he was the best entertainment in the cabin, she sat at the table with a drink and watched him prep. When he pulled raw chicken from the sink where it had been thawing, she raised her eyebrows. Hotdogs on a stick were one thing, but how was he going to cook chicken?

He worked quickly, cutting the chicken into small pieces and seasoning it with various things from the spice cabinet. He opened a can of mushrooms she'd bought to add to a frozen pizza and some bacon bits she used for salads.

Then he portioned it onto sheets of aluminum foil and folded them into packets. When he placed the packets directly on the brick in front of the roaring fire, Megan scoffed. He pointed at Libby and said, "Not for you." Then, he went back to the kitchen.

He sat down at the table with her with bright, smiling eyes. "Now, we wait." About ten minutes later, he turned the packets with a pair of tongs. After another ten minutes, he grabbed cheese from the fridge and carried it over to the fireplace. He pulled the packets away from the fire, but left them on the brick hearth. Then he seemed to nearly burn his fingers as he opened the packets and sprinkled in cheese. The smell of meat and seasoning hit her nose and her mouth began to water.

He closed them back up and went to get plates. When he finally dumped the contents of a pouch onto a plate and handed it to her with a fork, Megan leaned over and inhaled. "Okay, you win."

"You have to actually taste it first."

With a raised eyebrow, she replied, "I served you hotdogs and s'mores. You win."

He speared a forkful of smothered chicken and winked at her. "I know."

They ate his creation, and though the mushrooms were kind of briney, the steamed chicken was moist and tender. Adding bacon and cheese was a no-brainer and the whole thing was delicious.

When she'd eaten all she could handle, she offered the rest to Derek, who scraped it onto his own plate and finished it. "Would have been great with some mashed potatoes or something," he mused.

"Everything's better with mashed potatoes," she said with a laugh, laying down on her back to create space in her full stomach.

"True. Maybe when this is all done, we could go out for a real dinner. There is a restaurant called Evelyn's, have you tried it?" He set his empty plate on the coffee table and laid down on his side, propping his head up with his hand. Megan shook her head, and he replied,

"They have some of the best food in Freedom. Plus, it's in a cool old house."

"Sounds romantic."

"I suppose it is. Probably why I don't go there much. Is romantic okay with you?" Derek was looking down at her. Their fireplace picnic was over, and they were stretched out on the rug. His question hung in the air, and she simply nodded as he closed the distance between them and placed a lingering kiss on her lips.

The light faded on their second full day of being trapped together in this mountain cabin, and they stayed awake and whispered late into the night, wrapped in a cocoon of blankets to stay warm. In some ways, it felt more like a vacation than an inconvenience. She could imagine future vacations like this one, with Derek and cozy fireplace picnics.

A future like that would mean letting Derek into her life, though. Her real life. If this relationship had any chance of moving forward, she needed to come clean. But she'd been keeping the secret of her identity for so long, the thought of telling someone—even the man beside her in the dark—made a shiver run through her.

At her involuntary shudder, she felt Derek's arm tighten around her slightly and he murmured something unintelligible. Then, his breathing returned to the slow, steady pattern. She sighed into his embrace and promised herself she would tell him. Tomorrow.

13

Derek woke early, the sky still dim and the fire still going from when he'd stoked it late last night. Megan slept next to him, her brown hair fanned across the pillow. He leaned up on his elbow and traced a piece of it with his finger. She really was something special, and Derek couldn't imagine that after enduring this storm and surviving days with no outside contact and no one but each other that he would ever get tired of the beautiful woman next to him.

He slipped out from under the blankets and stretched as he stood. Whatever the reason, he was wide awake despite the early hour. Even Libby wasn't awake. Derek looked around the cabin, trying to decide his next move. The stairs to the loft seemed to beckon him and he stepped on to the first tread.

Voices within him waged war, one telling him to go back and lay down next to Megan—that snooping and digging could only cause problems. The other pushing him forward, up the stairs and to the notebook where answers might be found.

Derek took one step and then another until he stood in front of the small desk where Megan's laptop sat. Next to it, the plain black notebook. His fingers ran along the smooth cover, tracing the gilded letters that read simply "Notes."

He paused, listening for any sign of movement downstairs, but he heard none. He flipped open the notebook and skimmed the page before flipping to the next. Familiar names and places jumped out at him. Winters, Natalia, General Rutledge. He flipped to the next page. Jett Winters. Again, Jett. JW.

He covered his mouth to stifle the sharp intake of breath at his discovery. Megan wasn't writing romance. Megan Warren was Marcus Warner. His favorite author. Who very clearly had a picture of a middle-aged black man on the back cover of his books. Her books, he corrected himself. It was impossible. Wasn't it? But the notes were pretty undeniable. Mostly, they didn't make sense to him. Shorthand scribbles and fragmented sentences.

Derek sat down heavily in the chair, his mind still racing with the implications. Megan was Marcus Warner. At the bookstore, when he'd held her book. She hadn't told him. When he'd asked her about her project, she hadn't told him. So many chances to share and she hadn't.

Why wouldn't she tell him?

He'd known she was hiding something. Just like he knew the park ranger was hiding something when his sister went missing. Her evasive answers, the nervous laughter. All of it should have been a red flag, and he'd been too distracted by Megan's allure to listen to his gut. Instead of getting lost in those magnetic brown eyes and soft, kissable lips, he never should have gotten involved with her.

This was why he didn't trust people. He hated being lied to, and Megan had done it without a second thought. He was tired of being misled, and he wasn't going to let it happen again. He stood up, the chair scraped against the wood floor, and he couldn't seem to care.

He didn't try to quiet his heavy footsteps as he came down the stairs. When he reached the bottom, he saw a drowsy Megan sit up and rub her eyes. Liberty rose too and pushed her nose into Megan's neck, licking her cheek. Megan's soft laughter did nothing to soothe his anger and Derek tossed the black notebook he carried onto the blankets next to her.

Megan's wide eyes flew to his, and she scrambled to her feet.

"When were you going to tell me?"

"Why were you snooping through my things?" He pushed away the guilt at his sneaking around, and focused on the fact that he'd been right to do so.

"Apparently because I was correct when I thought you might be lying to me, Megan! Or should I say *Marcus*?" He sneered her fake name, and she shrank back.

"I wasn't ready to tell you, yet. This is my life. My *career!* It's none of your business. You can't just come in here and dig through my things. My life doesn't belong to you!" They were both yelling at this point and Libby whined, pacing the floor between them.

Derek shook his head. "You should have told me."

Megan grabbed a blanket and huddled on the couch. "You should have trusted me. I need you to leave. Call Pete and see when someone can come get you." Her tone left no room for argument, but he wanted to get out of there as much as she did.

He had a life to get back to. Dogs and a business. People who didn't lie to him about who they were. He marched to the phone on the wall and dialed Pete's number. A groggy voice greeted him, and he winced. The dim light outside told him it was still early.

"Hey, Petey. Sorry to wake you. It's Derek. Looking for an update on my exfil."

"Don't throw that military jargon at me at six in the morning, D. Give me a sec." When Pete came back, he sounded more awake. "Okay, looks like the snow plows ran through town, and they salted the roads. I'll have to see if there are any reports about the highway."

"That'd be great."

"What's the hurry? From what I heard, you and Megan ought to be snuggled by the fireplace." Derek clenched his jaw at the reminder.

"Yeah, well, we're not. So let me know."

"I'd say we can get you this afternoon. Plan on that unless I call you back, alright? I'll put Megan up at the lodge, too. Sounds like the power lines are down almost the entire way to the cabin, so it's unlikely she'll get power back anytime soon. She can finish her time in Freedom at the Lodge. I'll just need to call Kevin."

"Okay. I'll tell her to pack her things."

~

MEGAN TIPPED her head in confusion at his words as she listened to the one-sided conversation. Derek wrapped up the call with Pete and hung up. She waited expectantly and he gave her the rundown. His voice had taken on the serious, commanding tone she figured he used when directing volunteers on Search and Rescue missions. It left no room for argument and made her miss the light-hearted man she'd spent the last three days with.

That was the man who had snooped through her personal belongings, though. She shuddered. The memory of finding her clothes and journals strewn about her college dorm room was sharp in her mind. She hadn't caught Tristan in the act back then, but it was the incident that finally allowed her to get a restraining order against him. He refused to let go, and clearly didn't know personal boundaries.

Apparently Derek was the same way. She had woken up in such a good mood, cuddled up with Libby on the floor and the scent of Derek still on the blankets next to her.

She was going to tell him about Marcus today. But he hadn't given her the chance. She felt betrayed and exposed. It was a good thing Pete was coming to pick them up later today because she wasn't sure how long she would last.

Megan busied herself packing her clothes into the suitcases she'd stowed in the closet. She walked through the living room, grabbing books she'd purchased at Stories and Scones over the last few months. She found a box and grabbed snack foods from the cupboard that she could take to the Lodge. If Joanna was right, the place would be packed the week before Christmas. It would be a miracle if Megan could get any work done at all.

Finally, after a spoonful of peanut butter that passed for lunch, Megan sat at the table, her things neatly stacked by the door. Libby sat on her heels in front of her and laid her nose on Megan's lap. Her big, dark eyes looked up at Megan as though asking what went wrong.

"I don't know, girl," she whispered with a pat.

All morning, Derek had stomped around the cabin. He paced from window to window and moved from chair to chair. He'd put on the stiff, dirty clothes she'd found him in on her porch three nights ago. They'd barely exchanged two words since the fight.

A few questions from him about whether something was hers. Mostly, he talked to Libby or pouted in the corner. It was annoying, and Megan glanced out the window for the hundredth time, hoping to see a truck pulling up the snow-covered drive.

Derek came downstairs, and tossed her work bag on the table. At least he gently set the laptop down. How had she forgotten to get her things from upstairs? She stared at the black notebook still there, thinking of all the secrets it held. For a fan of Marcus Warner—a former fan, perhaps—there was a fortune to be made with what he'd seen. The true identity of the secretive best-selling author was one. Hints and snippets of the next Jett Winters books was another.

"Will you tell anyone?" Her voice was quiet, and she

was quite sure her desperation was plain in the quiver at the end.

"What?"

"You know something only four people in the entire world know. My parents, my sister, and my agent are the only ones who know that I am Marcus Warner."

Derek stared at her with raised eyebrows. "Seriously?"

She nodded slowly. "Yes. And it's important that it stays that way." Not only would she suddenly be thrust into the spotlight, but who knew what Tristan would do if she suddenly resurfaced after all this time.

"You would live your entire life in secrecy?"

She has been doing it for so long, it was hardly a question anymore. "You don't know anything about my life, Derek. But yes, I would. Unless you decide to tell the world who I am."

She saw the muscles in His jaw tense. "Whatever, Megan. I don't care that you are Marcus Warner, and I have better things to do than tell anyone." With that, Derek turned away and sat across the living room, suddenly interested in picking at something on his jeans.

Megan breathed a sigh of relief. "Thank you." Then, thoughts of her other concern bubbled up. "And the story? Will you share the storyline?"

He scoffed, "Megan, I have no idea what those notes meant. If there was a story in there, I don't know what it is. And I wouldn't share it if I did."

"Okay. Thank you." She looked out the window again, a huge silver truck with big tires and a snowplow on the front pulled into the clearing of the cabin. "Someone's here." Derek looked up from the fascinating threads of his jeans and nodded.

Megan turned back to the window and watched as the driver lowered the plow and pushed the snow across the driveway, making multiple passes until there was enough room to maneuver. Pete stepped down from the truck, his head covered with a black hat and his coat and scarf a fashionable combination. He held up an arm as he walked towards them. Megan quickly zipped her coat and pulled down her hat, then opened the front door to greet him.

"I bet you guys are ready for a hot meal!" Pete's friendly demeanor was a stark contrast to the tension in the cabin all morning, Megan found herself unable to respond.

Instead, she grabbed her suitcase and started toward the truck. "Here, let me get that," Pete insisted as he took it from her. Megan grabbed another load and followed him to the truck.

She tried to come up with something to say as she walked across the deep snow with Pete. "It's amazing how much more I'm leaving with than I came here with," she huffed. Libby ran past her, once again chasing the snow she was kicking into the air.

"I'm surprised you don't have more. Most people come to Freedom and spend a fortune at the shops on Main Street."

She laughed, "That's not really me."

Derek stepped past her, his long strides nearly twice as long as hers. "Pete, can you drop me at DK9? I'm assuming my Jeep will still be stuck."

Pete nodded. "Yeah, the highway is cleared, but I'm

sure they just pushed it onto that spur. I can drop you off and then get Megan settled at the lodge. Then, I'll swing back to get you, and I'll go help you get unburied."

Pete seemed like a great guy. Megan hoped the hints of a romance between him and Jan turned into something real. Just because she didn't write romance novels didn't mean she couldn't see the potential between the two of them. She didn't know Pete's story, but Jan deserved someone wonderful to share the rest of her life with.

Would Megan ever find that for herself? She had been so close to thinking Derek could be that person, but if he couldn't trust her enough to let her have her own space, it would never work.

It was better to find out now, than to let herself fall further in love with him.

As they all piled into Pete's oversized truck, Libby and Derek in the back, Megan put on a smile and fastened her seatbelt. She firmly ignored the feel of Derek's eyes on her.

14

*M*egan hadn't been back to Freedom Ridge Resort since the day she and Derek hiked to the falls. Joanna had mentioned that Megan should see it all decked out for Christmas, but Megan thought she had been exaggerating.

Pete pulled under the portico and Megan quickly realized that Joanna had not exaggerated at all. Freedom Ridge Resort wore the mantle of a mountain blizzard as though it was made for it. The white blanket on the gables and evergreen trees made the beautiful lodge look like something from a storybook. And then there were the giant wreaths on the door and the snowy garland with red bows decorating the stone pillars and benches around the small courtyard and firepits.

Inside was even more incredible, but the thing that hit Megan first was the warmth. She felt as though she hadn't been truly warm in three days, since the power went out. Derek's cold shoulder all day today certainly hadn't helped. But the fireplace inside the lodge was roaring and the lobby was lit with the warm glow of lamps and a large iron chandelier, not to mention the thousands of small twinkle lights that must be decorating not just one, but three Christmas trees she could see from where she stood.

Kevin walked up to them with a wide smile and held out his hand. "Welcome to Freedom Ridge, Ms. Warren. When Pete told me his cabin wouldn't have power for another week at least, I was more than happy to find you a room here."

"Are you sure it isn't an inconvenience?"

"Absolutely! With that storm, we had a slew of cancellations anyway, so there's a wonderful room with your name on it."

Kevin ushered her toward the front desk and Pete promised to check in on her the following day. Kevin stopped in front of the desk, "Debby, could you check Ms. Warren in? Her reservation should be under Pete's account. Send Trevor up ahead with her bags so she can get settled." He pulled open his suit jacket and grabbed something from the interior pocket. "I'm sure you're hungry and tired, so here are a few things to help with that. Dinner is on us at the Liberty Grille, and here are a few drink vouchers for something hot from the Mountain Mug." He pointed to the red logo above a coffee counter across the lobby. "Let me or Debby here know if you need anything else during your stay."

With that, he was off and Megan was left in a daze, watching him go. "Didn't y'all lose power during the storm?" she asked Debby.

Debby gave her a warm smile. "We did, but Kevin had

them fire up the generator. No place I'd rather be in a blizzard than stuck at Freedom Ridge."

Megan hummed her agreement and Debby gave her the room key and a brochure. After so many weeks in the solitude of the cabin and the last three days with only the light of the fire or a flashlight, the noise and lights of the resort were a bit overwhelming. However, she would brave the stimulation of the lobby if it meant she could get a cup of coffee, so she went over to the coffee bar and redeemed one of Kevin's vouchers for the largest cup of coffee she could order.

The first sip scalded her tongue, but by the time she reached her hotel room, she was gulping the hot beverage and enjoying the heat as it settled in her stomach. Three days without a warm cup of coffee was three days too many.

She opened the door from the quiet hallway, grateful that the bustle of the lobby seemed contained to the common space. Her room was spacious and included a small sofa and coffee table. The lodge feeling downstairs-- the stone fireplace and dark wooden beams--was echoed in the room. A small stone accent wall emphasized the small kitchenette, and the floor was a dark wood.

With a heavy sigh, she collapsed on the bed's crisp white duvet, and pulled up the soft brown throw blanket from the edge. Rolling over onto her stomach, she released the tears that had been trying to fall all day.

∾

DEREK USUALLY ENJOYED the chaotic welcome he got from his dogs. Today, he didn't think he had ever been more grateful to hear their playful barks. DK9 was a large facility near the outskirts of town, with indoor and outdoor areas for the dogs, in addition to their kennels. At any given time, Derek had about 10-15 dogs between the breeding, basic training, and specialized training operations.

Derek found Jared leading the dogs through an obstacle course, and he could tell the dogs close to graduation from the pups just by how they reacted to his entrance. Dobby was the first to him, his energetic tail wagging made Derek smile, even though it reminded him of Dobby finding his way to Megan's front porch, much like Derek had during the blizzard.

Other dogs greeted Liberty more than they greeted him, and his loyal companion took off to greet Jared as he walked toward them. "Good to see you, man. You had me worried."

"Me too," he admitted. A few times over the last three days, he'd realized just how close he'd been to freezing to death in the snow. It was a surreal knowledge, that a few steps in the wrong direction, or if Liberty had succumbed to the cold before he did and hadn't been able to get Megan's attention? It would have been the end of Derek Held.

For whatever reason, God decided it wasn't time yet. And Derek wanted to make the most of the time he was given. Which meant pushing aside any lingering thoughts about the beautiful writer he'd slept next to last night and focusing on his business and purpose.

Whatever the reason Megan had needed to lie to him, he wasn't going to try to take things any further with a woman who could be dishonest to him for so long. Even if she was intelligent and had the sexiest southern accent.

Clearly it wasn't meant to be. Besides, she was going home next week anyway.

Derek caught up with his business partner about the last few days. "Thanks for staying here with them, Jared. I'm sure Melody wasn't thrilled about that."

Jared's pained expression made Derek pause and raise an eyebrow. "Yeah, Melody left. She called me from Sacramento the night of the blizzard, apparently got the last flight before the storm shut down the airport."

"She just left without telling you?" Melody and Jared had been getting pretty serious.

"Yep. She said she had some things to sort out before she could settle down with someone like me."

"Aw, man. I'm sorry. Did she know about the engagement ring?" Jared had planned to propose on Christmas Eve.

"I don't think so? But maybe that's what got her spooked?"

Derek patted his friend's shoulder. "I don't know man, but if her reaction to finding out about a ring was to leave town so fast she left her shadow behind, maybe it's for the best."

"Enough about Melody. How was being snowed-in with the cute writer. I've got a ring that needs a good home," he added with a sarcastic bite.

Derek waved a hand, "Next topic. It was no big deal. Just a place to wait out the storm."

Jared frowned at him. "Are you sure? Isn't she the girl you went hiking with? And who found Dobby?"

"Yep. Same one. Come on, let's run a quick test on Payton." The drug-detecting dog was almost ready to graduate. Which is how he referred to it when he sold the dogs, because it seemed too business-like to think of it as selling his four-legged-friends.

After he changed into a set of spare clothes from his office, Derek set up a quick inspection run for Payton. He hid the drug scent in three of the boxes, while Jared and the dog went into another room. Although Jared tried to push the conversation further, Derek had shifted into business mode and ignored his questions.

He didn't want to talk about the days he spent with Megan in the cabin. While it had been cozy and happy, in the end, his own suspicions had been correct, and Megan had been a liar. Libby brought a toy to him and set it at his feet while he watched Jared and Payton complete the course. He petted the sweet dog. At least one woman in his life loved him.

15

The lodge turned out to be a welcome change from the cabin. Room service was something she could definitely get used to. Megan did venture down for dinner one evening, but eating by herself at the hotel restaurant wasn't exactly fun. The restaurant was full of families on vacation and couples enjoying candlelit dinners.

She sat at the bar and watched some sort of football game on the TV above the bartender's head. Occasionally, she turned toward the windows to enjoy the stunning mountain view, a bigger version of the view from her room upstairs. Unlike her view at the cabin, this view was entirely unobscured by trees and the windows perfectly framed the rest of the mountain range.

The bartender set her plate in front of her, a hearty serving of the creamy pasta that was tonight's special. Megan read her nametag quickly and said, "Thanks, Beth."

"My pleasure."

Megan sat and ate her pasta, her trusty black notebook

sitting unopened next to her as she thought about the story. Jett was in a tight spot, forced to trust someone who had betrayed him before and Megan was finding his struggle was falling flat. Perhaps because she didn't believe it. Why would Jett trust Natalia? Their history was complicated — the entire basis for her first book.

Natalia had betrayed Jett. But if he didn't trust her now, he would lose everything. As Megan sat and slowly prepped herself for a carb-induced coma, her thoughts shifted from Jett and Natalia to her and Derek.

Derek has betrayed her, but what would she lose if she didn't give him another chance? Could she, like Jett, put herself out there and try again? If she apologized to Derek for the secret, would he give her a second chance? Was she Natalia in this scenario? Or Jett?

Megan flipped open her notebook and started hitting down the emotions she felt when she considered trusting Derek again. That's what she needed to convey for Jett. If she could communicate her thoughts in the manuscript, she hoped it could help her tell Derek how she felt as well. She knew she needed to apologize. Her own fear had stopped her, even though Derek had given her every reason to trust him.

God brought him to her porch in the middle of the storm, the perfect opportunity to open up and let someone in. But she had closed herself off.

She wasn't going to make that mistake again. First, she needed to finish her book. The editor was already waiting for it. She'd try to call Derek before she had to leave, but going home for Christmas wasn't actually optional. She said a quick prayer that he would at least give her a chance to make things right.

Beth boxed up the leftover pasta for her and Megan went back upstairs. She needed to make sure Jett forgave Natalia. And while she was at it, she would work on getting Derek to forgive her.

16

*T*he week leading up to Christmas, Derek ignored a handful of calls from Megan, convinced it was better if he just let her leave and tried to move on with his life.

Between his mom's lack of interest and his closest friends having cozy Christmases with their families, Derek was feeling pretty sorry for himself. Reluctantly, he grabbed the gift card for Stories and Scones that he was contributing to the men's gift exchange and headed to men's Bible Study. He caught up with Clifford, the owner of Freedom Ridge, at the front door and opened it for the old man. Clifford was well into his eighties, and Derek loved talking to the old man. "Merry Christmas, Mr. Harrington."

"Call me Cliff, Derek. I've told you that."

"I know, sir." Derek had no intention of calling the revered elder of their church by anything other than Mr. Harrington. "How are you?"

"Oh, as well as an 85 year old man can be, I suppose.

My grandson, Bryce, is coming for Christmas this year, should get here tomorrow."

"That's great. Christmas should be spent with family."

As though he could hear the melancholy hidden in Derek's cheerful words, Clifford paused his slow, cane-assisted walk down the hallway and turned toward Derek. "And who will you be spending the holiday with, my boy?"

Derek flushed. "Umm, I'm not really sure yet."

Clifford watched him and then nodded, "Hmm. Maybe I should ask who you'd like to spend it with instead." Instead of asking, he turned around and kept walking, soon entering the conference room where the men's group waited and Christmas music played softly.

Derek knew who he wanted to spend Christmas with. Her face hadn't left his mind since he left the cabin four days ago. Every time he looked at his bookshelf at home, he got angry. When he got home, he had taken his Marcus Warner books and chucked them in the spare bedroom. Now, the gap they left behind on the shelf mocked him each time he saw it.

Despite four days to let it sink in, he still had a hard time with the reality that Megan was his favorite author. He had so many questions, but he was also stubbornly set on letting her go. She had misled him, and he wasn't ready to let that go.

He stepped into the conference room to greetings from his friends, Aiden, Carson, and Max. Aiden and Carson both worked for the fire station and could only come to Bible study when it fit their shift schedule. Max was a police officer in town.

"Merry Christmas, guys. How's it going?"

Aiden was the first to speak up. "Joanna is pregnant!"

"Oh, wow! That's awesome, Aiden. Congratulations! I bet your mom is over the moon."

Aiden gave a guilty smile. "Actually, she doesn't know yet. Her Christmas present is some sort of Grandma gear that Jo picked out."

Derek rolled his eyes along with the rest of the guys. "Women are weird."

Max nodded, "That's for sure. Have I told you that Thea is back in town?"

"Thea Riley?" Aiden confirmed.

"Yep. Housesitting. But we've been spending a lot of time together. During the storm, she got iced in at the secondary event center at the resort."

Max continued to fill them in and Derek could see the stars in his eyes. He said a quick prayer that his friend wouldn't end up hurt again. From what he knew of Thea and Max's story, Max might not survive it if she left again.

The men's group was good, a short devotional about Christmas and then a ridiculous gifting game in which Derek ended up with--of course--a Marcus Warner novel. Was God trying to mess with him or something?

He went back to DK9 to let the dogs run around for a while, and he grabbed his Bible and sat in the makeshift living room on the edge of the indoor recreation space. The dogs chased each other, occasionally Dobby or Ruby would bring him a tennis ball, and he would throw it and watch as the dogs tripped over each other to retrieve it.

Derek had a good life, all things considered. When his sister went missing and his parents went off the rails, it would have been easy for him to fall through the cracks. But thanks to the family of his best friend growing up, Derek had a support system. He needed to call his buddy, Ryan again soon. They'd both joined the army together, but after that it was hit or miss when they found time to hang out.

Without Aiden and his parents, Derek could have followed his own parents down the depressing spiral of drugs and alcohol. Strong faith and a lot of therapy had gotten him to a place where he could lead a happy life. And if that life didn't include Megan, that was going to be okay.

He sat and flipped through his Bible, unsure what he was looking for within its pages. Less than a week ago, he'd almost died. Was it unreasonable to wonder why? Was it morbid to consider perhaps it should have ended differently. Probably. What was it that Jesus said? *I have come so they would have life to the fullest.*

What did that look like for Derek? Probably not questioning every decent person he ran into, or snooping through his friends' medicine cabinets looking for hidden drug habits. The remnant said of the trust issues his parents had given him were hard to let go of. Even when he knew he needed to.

Christmas Eve was in a few days. Megan was leaving, but next time he wouldn't make the same mistake. He needed God to help him trust and let God take control. Derek didn't have to protect himself so vigorously, because God would protect him as well.

It was probably too late for things to work out with

Megan. With the way he'd invaded her privacy, she was probably calling him to have him sign some sort of legal form about what he'd seen. He'd been wrong to intrude, but that ship had sailed. If only he could stop thinking about her.

17

___

Three days before Christmas, Megan packed her suitcase and with one final look into the hotel room, shut the door behind her. In the last five days, she had majorly reworked her story, and she was confident she was delivering the best possible Jett Winters story to her editor.

Derek hadn't answered any of her calls. Megan was trying to be okay with that and chalk it up to lessons learned, but the rejection still stung. She handed her key to Debby at the front desk, and then pulled a large, thick envelope from her laptop bag.

"Debby, could I leave this here for someone?"

"Of course, Ms. Warren."

"If Derek Held comes in before New Year's, would you give it to him? Otherwise, please shred the contents."

Debby raised an eyebrow. "Are you sure, Megan?"

She must really be surprised to slip out of her always-professional demeanor. Megan nodded, "I'm sure. New Year's Eve."

"Alright." Megan watched as Debby jotted on a sticky note and pressed it firmly on the orange envelope. Her entire heart had been poured onto those pages, and if Derek read them, maybe he would understand. She'd figured it out. She was Natalia, and she desperately needed Derek to forgive her so they could save the world. Or, in this case, their relationship.

Megan climbed into her car which Pete had managed to safely deliver from the cabin to the lodge, and started the 22-hour drive back to Alabama.

Two days and one hotel night later, Megan pulled into the familiar driveway in the perfectly ordinary subdivision outside of Birmingham. She knew the sunny December weather would have her family in coats, but she stepped out of the car in just a T-shirt. Three months in the mountains had thickened her skin. Or perhaps it had been the three days without power.

She stepped through the door and was immediately engulfed in the warm embrace of her mother. Tracie was close behind and Megan relished the physical contact and familiar faces.

"I missed y'all so much!" she said honestly.

"Come in, come in. You must be exhausted!"

"I really am. I'm happy as a clam at high tide to be home, though."

Her Dad and Uncle busied themselves unloading her car and Megan wandered into the kitchen, where preparations were underway for Christmas dinner tomorrow. She sat at the bar and watched as Tracie mixed the batter for a cheesecake and her mom iced Christmas cookies. It was a picture-perfect family Christmas, but Megan couldn't help but feel something was missing. Maybe she was just tired. Twenty-two hours on the road was enough to put anyone in a strange mood.

The next morning, though, Megan tried her best to enjoy the festivities. They exchanged gifts, and Megan proudly presented her family the things she'd gotten for them in Freedom. For Tracie, a hand-poured pine-scented candle from Wick and Sarcasm, the candle-shop on Main Street. She had picked a hand-blown vase for her mom and an old-fashioned oil lantern for her dad who loved antiques. And for the extended family, a sampler pack from Freedom Fudge Factory.

With each gift that they unwrapped, Megan felt the pull of the small, picturesque town. Three months she had lived there, and Freedom had welcomed her like one of their own. From Jan at Stories and Scones, to Pete and his beautiful cabin, and Derek.

As her mom handed around glasses of eggnog, Tracie sat on the couch beside her. "What's wrong, sis?"

Megan widened her eyes and played dumb, "What do you mean? It's Christmas, how could something be wrong?"

Tracie wasn't buying it. "Nice try. Now, tell me why you look like you'd trade that brand new ereader for a ticket back to Freedom. And don't try to convince me it's the fudge, even though Uncle Garrett let me try a piece of his and it's definitely worth the plane ticket."

Megan smiled tightly. "I don't know, Trace. There was this guy..."

"I'm listening," her sister prodded.

"Derek and I got to know each other pretty well, but

we both sort of agreed that there was no use pursuing anything further. So we hung out as friends while I was in town. And then there was this huge blizzard and he almost died in the snow but ended up at my cabin."

Tracie's eyes were as big as the oversized ornaments on the Christmas tree. "Like… snowed in together?"

"Yeah. But it wasn't exactly glamorous. The power went out, and we were there with a dog and no way to cook food. Except that Derek was pretty good with these foil packet things."

"Whoa, whoa, whoa. Derek cooked for you? How long were you stranded together?"

"Three days," Megan admitted.

"Three days! And you didn't call to tell me? Wait, is this the guy who took you to the waterfall?"

Megan nodded.

"Girl!" Tracie drew out the word and Megan smiled at her dramatic nature. They couldn't be more different. "So why are you so sad? Do you just miss him? When do you go back?"

"I'm not going back, Tracie. Our little blizzard adventure didn't exactly have a happy ending. He found out who I was and was furious that I had lied to him."

Tracie leaned back against the couch. "Oh. As in… Marcus?"

"Yes. Marcus. And I tried to call him before I left, but he wouldn't take any of my calls."

"Oh, I'm sorry, sweetie. Did you try to go see him?"

Megan shook her head. "No, I didn't have the nerve. Plus, I was trying to finish my book. There wasn't enough time!"

"Okay, I get it. But you've got to go back. You've got to apologize and make him understand. You can't give up! I've never heard you talk about someone the way you talked about the waterfall guy with the puppies."

Megan laughed at her sister's description of Derek. "What if he doesn't forgive me?" She whispered the question and her sister's arms came around her.

"Then you'll come back home, and we'll buy some ice cream and adopt a puppy together. But at least you'll know that you did everything you could do."

Derek spent Christmas Eve with Aiden, Joanna, and Jan. They were the closest thing he had to family in Freedom Ridge and thankfully had always included him. Between Aiden's family and Carson's family, Derek had no lack of offers for holiday plans.

They went to Christmas Eve service together and then had dinner at Jan's house. He couldn't help but smile watching Jan open up her personalized "Promoted to Grandma" t-shirt from Aiden and Joanna, and the picture of the ultrasound was pretty cool, even though the baby mostly looked like a smudge on the paper to him.

"When are you due?" Jan asked once the tears had subsided and the hugs had been exchanged.

Joanna glanced at Aiden before answering, "July. We are only a few months along, but we couldn't wait to share the news! No one else knows yet, and we will tell my family next week when we're in Arizona."

Derek gave Aiden a congratulatory hug, slapping him

on the back. He let Aiden know with a wink that he wouldn't reveal how Aiden shared their secret at Men's Group. "Excited for you guys. You know what every kid needs, right?"

Aiden raised his eyebrows and replied, "A snowboard?"

His smart-aleck response earned him a good-natured glare from Joanna.

"Nah. A puppy! Just think, you get it now and by the time the baby comes, it'll be the perfect companion."

"I don't think so, D. I plan to enjoy my sleep while I can get it," Joanna replied with a grin.

"Oh fine, but when Aiden Jr. wants a dog, you know where to come."

"See, I told you Aiden Jr. was a good name!" Aiden joked with his wife and pulled her in for a hug.

Derek took his leave soon after that. He drove around in his Jeep for a bit, surprising himself when he turned up the drive to Pete's cabin where Megan had stayed. Unsurprisingly, the cabin was dark, since Megan's reservation should have lasted through Christmas. His headlights reflected back from the windows and though the snow was still lingering, it had started to melt some.

He didn't know what he was hoping to find here. Derek knew Megan wasn't in Freedom. And even if she were, she wouldn't be here at the cabin. She would be at the lodge. His phone buzzed with a low battery alert, and he stared at the tiny red notification on his voicemails. Megan had left him one the other day. She'd called several times, but he'd never answered, and she'd never left a message. Until now.

Hesitantly, he pulled the phone to his ear and pressed play.

The sound of Megan's sweet Alabama twang made his chest physically hurt. He shouldn't miss her this much. Her words made his heart rate accelerate.

"Hey Derek. Look, I'm really sorry about what happened. I, uhh, I'm leaving something for you at the lodge. Debby will know how to get it if you stop by. I really hope you will."

Despite the small storm that was brewing, Derek drove as quickly as he could to Freedom Ridge Resort, pulling under the portico and parking near the curb at the far side. He could move it later. Right now, he needed to find Debby.

He ran through the doors and looked around the lounge, his eyes landing on the front desk where Debby stood at her usual station. He'd never been more grateful for her workaholic tendency to take all the overtime she could.

"Derek, I was starting to wonder if I would see you."

"Do you have it?"

Debby smiled and held up a finger. "Let me go get it from the safe."

The safe? What on earth could Megan have left for him that needed to be kept in the Resort's safe? Debby came back holding an orange folder, like one he would mail documents in.

She handed it across the counter to him. "I don't know what this is, but Megan seemed very adamant that it was either to go to you or be shredded."

His curiosity flared further and Derek headed to the

nearest seat, an overstuffed leather armchair near the fireplace. He carefully opened the clasp on the folder and slid a stack of papers nearly an inch thick out. On top, he found a sticky note.

Derek, I desperately want to let you in. Pay close attention to pages 141-150. Love, M.W.

Under the sticky note, the words "Jett Winters, Untitled Book 5, Manuscript Draft, Confidential" jumped out at him in stark black letters. She'd given him the entire book?

Derek shifted in the chair and removed his coat. Then, he flipped to the first page.

18

-----

*D*erek spared a glance and a smile as Debby brought him a cup of coffee. He knew it was probably well after midnight and that he'd been reading for hours. Not another soul stirred in the lounge where he'd remained firmly camped. There was little else he would rather be doing than reading Megan's newest book.

Not only did he recognize the big step it had been for her to share it with him, knowing that he could, if he chose, sell it to the highest bidder or splash it across the internet. It meant she trusted him.

Plus, he just loved the Jett Winters books. When he'd seen Natalia's name in the notes, Derek figured he was looking at old notes, but the last few hours of reading revealed Natalia was back in Jett's life. Derek glanced at the page number. He was almost to the pages Megan pointed out.

When he got to them, he saw that she had highlighted portions. His eyes skipped to the first highlighted portion. It was an apology from Natalia, begging for forgiveness from Jett. He moved to the next portion. Jett considered if he could trust her after betrayal. The scene continued and Derek read, breathless as he saw Megan's struggle to reveal her true self to him written on the pages.

Megan took Jett and Natalia through the wringer, hashing out their complicated past and ultimately, using it to draw them together. Derek said a prayer that it could work the same for them.

He finished reading, two more hours in which he barely moved from his chair. Fighting the yawns, he flipped to the final page and spotted the inscription.

This book is dedicated to Derek, whom I would trust with all my secrets.

The grin that broke on Derek's face could have been a mixture of pure joy and lack of sleep, but Derek didn't care. If there had been anyone in the lounge to see him, he would have looked like a crazy person. He was alone though, and didn't bother trying to contain it.

"So, is she coming back?"

Derek's head swiveled toward the voice and he realized that Debby was sitting across the lounge at a small table with Drew, the night security guard. She waited, eyebrows raised, and then asked again. "Well, is she?"

He stood up and walked towards them. "I actually don't know. But I'm pretty sure I'm going to her."

Debby gave a dreamy sigh and swooned, "That's so romantic!" Derek chuckled and Drew rolled his eyes. "What are you waiting for? Go!" Debby shooed him away and Derek climbed back in his Jeep. Libby would be waiting for him at home, and one of the assistant trainers was taking care of all the dogs tonight, whereas he was supposed to handle them on Christmas Day.

Maybe Jared would be able to cover for him. Fifteen minutes later, Derek pulled into his driveway. Once he was inside, he let Libby out and pulled up his laptop, browsing flights to Birmingham for tomorrow. He checked the clock. It was 4 AM and some of the flights were leaving in just a few hours. Libby came back to the door, and he shut the laptop. His best bet would be to take care of everything he needed to and then just book a flight whenever he was able to make it to the airport. First, he did actually need to sleep--at least for an hour or two. When he woke up, he'd try to call Megan. If he was going to show up on Christmas Day, he was going to need an address.

MEGAN CLOSED her suitcase in the trunk of her car, feeling like she had just pulled it out. Hugging her parents and sister who were still in their pajamas, she said goodbye.

"Are you sure I shouldn't wait? It's Christmas. I feel like I should be here."

"Megan, you've never done something spontaneous in your whole life. Go. Find Derek and make things right. We can't wait to meet the man who finally broke through those walls of yours." Megan's mom was kind but firm in her instruction.

"Thanks, Mom. I'll call you when I land."

She drove into the early morning sun and parked at

the airport. At least she didn't have a twenty-two hour drive ahead of her. With the ticket she had booked last night, she would land in Denver just after ten.

The airport wasn't busy, and she made it through security, being extra sure to be friendly to all the workers giving up their holiday. Impatiently, she waited for her flight to board. Once she was in her first-class seat, Megan obediently turned off her cell phone and settled in for the 3-hour flight.

She felt a little crazy, but at the same time, Megan knew she was doing the right thing. God had been working on her the last three months. Every time she attempted to shut Derek out, God had thrown him right back in her path. And while trusting people didn't come easily to her, He was showing her that there are people worth being trusted - most of all, God Himself.

I'm sorry I've been trying to do everything myself. I don't want to be closed off and cynical. Help me see the goodness around me and in people in my life. Help me make things right with Derek.

Her prayers throughout the flight and the drive remained similar. God was good and wanted good things for her. She just had to say yes to Him.

THE RINGTONE of Derek's phone woke him up and he groggily reached for the nightstand to silence the obnoxious noise. A bleary-eyed look at the screen showed Jared's name. "Yeah?" he croaked into the phone once he had answered.

"Hey, D. Sorry to wake you. Merry Christmas, by the way. I've got bad news." Derek opened his eyes and stared at the ceiling.

"Slow down, Jared. What's going on?"

"Amber called me this morning. She can't find Dobby. Apparently, his gate didn't latch, and he snuck out in the storm last night"

"I'm sure he's just sleeping on one of the couches in the office or something."

"I'm already here, D. We've searched the building, and he is nowhere to be found."

Derek groaned. "Okay. I'll be there in twenty minutes." He rubbed his eyes, and Libby whined and laid her head on the edge of the bed. "Make that twenty-five." He knew the drive to DK9 would take him exactly seven minutes if the roads were clear. Libby would come with him, but she needed a chance to eat, and he needed a shower.

Twenty-two minutes later, Derek parked in front of DK9 and found Jared already waiting outside for him. "What's the plan?" he asked his friend and business partner.

"He's gotta be outside somewhere. I say we check the houses over in Ash Ridge." The subdivision backed up to the DK9 property.

"Yeah, okay. Just remember that it's Christmas. Where's Amber?"

"She's afraid you're going to fire her," Jared admitted with a chuckle.

Derek scowled. "It's not her fault Dobby is basically an out-of-control toddler who can run twenty miles an hour. Get her out here and have her call anyone else who can help." He looked back at his Jeep where Liberty was waiting. "I'll start at the west side and work my way down Ashbury and Woodbury."

Jared nodded and promised to divvy up the remaining streets in the subdivision with everyone else. Derek climbed back in the Jeep and pulled out of the parking lot. "This was not what I was supposed to be doing today, Libby. I should be on my way to Birmingham by now."

Libby barked in response.

"I know, I know. It'll all work out. I just miss her."

Two hours later, there was no sign of Dobby in the neighborhood. Jared, Amber, and Amber's boyfriend Chase stood in the center of a cul-de-sac. "Maybe he went toward town instead."

"Just a second," Amber said as she pulled out her phone. "I've been checking all morning, but there was nothing. But look! She turned her phone toward Derek. He gave the young girl a blank look instead of studying the screen.

"Why don't you just tell me?"

"Someone just posted on the Freedom Ridge Community page saying they saw a dog running around near the Courthouse when they were driving."

"It's got to be Dobby. Let's go."

MEGAN HAD DRIVEN the now-familiar route from Denver and pulled into Freedom around noon. Christmas Day meant the town square was uncharacteristically quiet, and Megan parked in front of Stories and Scones, even though it was closed. The towering Christmas Tree was lit up in the courtyard. Though the snow and ice had been cleared from all the sidewalks, there were tracks of footsteps through the unmelted snow on the grass.

Motion near the base of the Christmas tree caught her eye, and Megan looked closer. There was something moving near the nativity set at the base of the tree. A flash of gold and brown had her stepping out of her car in curiosity.

Suddenly, the blur of brown started running toward her. It was a dog! She instinctively looked left and right to make sure no one was going to run it over, then bent down as the dog reached her. What was Dobby doing here?

Looking around for any sign of Derek, Megan kept a hand on Dobby's collar. "Hey, sweet boy. Where's your daddy? Huh? I was looking for him." There was no sign of Derek, though. Megan walked with Dobby back to the Christmas Tree, wondering if there was some explanation. But when she got there, she found only the hay from the Nativity Scene strewn about where Dobby had apparently been playing.

She walked over to the gazebo and sat on the steps, her hand still on Dobby. The dog seemed perfectly content to stay with her, leaning against Megan's knees and licking her hand. Megan's gaze roamed around the courtyard again, still searching for Derek.

An SUV pulled onto Main Street and her heart skipped at the sight of a familiar logo on the side. The Jeep parked across three of the diagonal spaces, near her own in front of Stories and Scones. Dobby tugged and

Megan held his collar tightly. "He's coming, boy." This was it. Seeing Derek was why she'd come back. Had he gone to the lodge? What if he didn't want to see her?

Finally, when he was across the street, Megan released Dobby and watched with a laugh as the energetic German Shepherd tore across the park. Derek barely acknowledged the dog, but continued toward her place on the gazebo step. She stood, silently repeating the prayers she'd been reciting since she left Freedom Ridge only four days before. Dobby ran circles around him, barking happily at being reunited with his owner.

Derek's eyes remained locked on her, but called over his shoulder, "Jared?" It was only then that Megan noticed another truck had parked on the street next to the courtyard. "Take care of Dobby," he instructed.

A whistle got Dobby's attention and the dog raced toward Jared and the waiting treat. Derek continued his unveering course toward her, his expression impossible to read. Her heart was in her throat as she met the piercing stare of his gorgeous blue eyes. She wanted to leap into his arms, but she still didn't know how he felt or if he'd ever even listened to her message. What was she thinking just showing up here unannounced? Maybe this was a mistake.

And then, Derek said her name.

19

*H*e thought it was a dream when he'd seen Dobby with her across the park. Perhaps a hallucination brought on by lack of sleep. Normally, he would have given Dobby the attention the pup deserved, but he'd been unable to focus on anything except the beautiful woman standing in the park.

She was really here. And suddenly, all the things he wanted to say were lost.

"Megan," he breathed.

"Hi. I tried to call," she said shyly.

"I'm sorry--"

"Did you get--"

They both cut off their words, and Derek reached for her hands. "I got your message. I read the book last night."

"The whole thing?"

"Every word. I'm so sorry I expected you to share all of your secrets with me without giving us the time to get there. I'm especially sorry for how I violated your trust and privacy."

Megan was shaking her head, and she squeezed his fingers. "I'm sorry for shutting you out of that part of my life. I've kept it a secret for so long, the idea of sharing it with anyone was terrifying."

It was Derek's turn to shake his head. "I shouldn't have pushed."

"I should have trusted you. I *do* trust you." Hearing those words filled him with warmth, followed immediately by regret.

"Maybe you shouldn't trust me. My sister trusted me, and I let her down with tragic results. What if I'm not worthy of this trust?"

Megan stepped close and looked up at him. "Derek, it was never your fault that your sister went missing. Her trust in you was never misplaced, and neither is mine. You are, without a doubt, one of the most honorable men I've ever known."

"And you, Megan Warren, are the most talented author, most beautiful woman, and most charming neat freak I know." He was trying to make her smile, and apparently it worked because the chuckle she gave him was exactly what he'd been missing for two weeks. Unable to resist any longer, he leaned down to press his lips to hers. In the cold of the day, her lips were warm and sweet. He dropped one hand and wrapped his arm around her waist, pulling her closer into him.

He held her, tasting her and soaking in the miracle that was Megan--here, on Christmas Day. "I can't believe you're here," he whispered with a smile, then traced a lock of hair that trailed by her cheek with his finger, tucking it behind her ear.

"I had to come. I couldn't wait for a call that might never come. And Tracie told me I was being an idiot, so there was that."

He smiled, "I think I like your sister already." Then, he lowered his mouth to hers again. All the pieces of himself that had felt disjointed and heavy since he left her cabin fell into place. The towering Christmas tree twenty feet away could have burst into flames and he might not have noticed, because there was nothing as all-consuming as her lips on his and her body wrapped in his arms.

When he broke the kiss again, it was because of the urgent nudge near his knee. "What the--Dobby!" Derek looked up to see Jared jogging across the park, trying to get Dobby's attention.

Megan threw her head back and laughed. "I think Dobby is just celebrating. After all, he had a bit to do with our being together."

Derek shook his head. "This dog will be the end of me. There is no way he can cut it as a working dog."

Megan lowered to the ground and hugged the playful dog around the neck. She looked up at Derek and said, "Perhaps Dobby doesn't need to be a working dog. Maybe he could just be my dog." Then she added with hesitation. "Or our dog?"

Her adoration of his dogs, plus her cheery smile and pink-tinged nose had him tempted to drop to a knee next to her and ask the kind of question a man was only supposed to ask on bended knee. But he wouldn't do that yet. He was impulsive, but Megan was careful. And working out the details together would be an important step.

"I think Dobby would be a perfect family dog."

Megan's smile beamed, and he knew he'd said exactly the right thing.

"See Dobby? You can come home with me." The dog began to sing in response, making them both laugh.

Jared reached them, panting slightly. "Sorry about that. Dobby's a tricky one. Here, I can take him."

Megan shook her head and left her hand on Dobby's collar, where once again he was content to stand still. Derek just laughed. "I think Dobby has decided who he wants to belong to, and it isn't you and me, Jared. Jared, this is Megan. Megan, this is Jared, my business partner."

They shook hands and Jared gave him a not-so-subtle look complete with goofy eyebrow wiggle. Derek playfully swatted a hand toward the back of his friends head before sending him on his way. "Thanks for tracking down Dobby with me. You can just go ahead and call it a day. Have a Merry Christmas."

"Nice to meet you, Megan. It would seem I might be seeing you around a lot more."

"Goodbye, Jared." Megan laughed softly as Jared walked back toward his truck. "He seems fun."

Derek pulled her back into his arms again. "I'm fun, too."

Megan laughed and snuggled into his arms. "Merry Christmas, Derek."

He kissed the top of her head, and they started walking toward their cars. "Merry Christmas, Megan."

EPILOGUE

*N*ew Years Eve brought with it an impromptu party. Megan saw familiar faces such as Jan from the coffee shop and Haven from the lodge. But Derek clearly knew everyone.

"Max! I hear congratulations are in order?" Derek shook the hand of a handsome man, with his arm tucked around the waist of a blonde woman.

"Derek, good to see you. Yes, this is my wife Thea. Thea, this is Derek Held. He was a few years ahead of us in school, but he started a dog training facility here in town years back. And who is this?"

Max turned his blue eyes to Megan, and she blushed. Derek's arm around her waist tightened. "This is Megan Warren, my girlfriend."

Max's eyebrows lifted. "I guess Thea isn't the only one who had an eventful blizzard two weeks ago."

It seemed like months had passed since she found Derek and Liberty on her doorstep in the snow. So much had changed since that night. Derek knew her secret, for one. Even more important? She loved him and trusted him with all of her secrets moving forward.

Derek filled her in on Max and Thea's story, "Thea got stuck at the secondary event center at the lodge. Luckily Max hunted her down. When was the wedding?" he asked Max.

"Just a few days ago. After that little storm that blew through Christmas Eve, we had to wait a few days. But we didn't want to wait too long," he said with a twinkle of laughter. The couple looked so adorably in love, Megan almost sighed.

Max and Thea drifted off to talk to someone else, just as the trill of someone striking glass got the attention of everyone in the room. She whispered to Derek, "That's Aiden, right?" They'd had coffee with Aiden and Joanna the other day. Derek nodded.

"I have an announcement," Aiden spoke over those who were still talking. "Many of you already know that Joanna is expecting our first child," —murmurs from people in the crowd rose, and he spoke louder— "What we just found out ourselves is that it is going to be a baby boy!"

Cheers and applause rang through the room, and Aiden stepped down from the chair he'd been standing on.

When Haven came up, Megan made the connection. "Hello Haven, you look beautiful!" It wasn't an exaggeration, either. Haven's sequined dress hugged her curves, including the perfect baby bump protruding from her small frame. "Jeremiah, remember how I was telling you about Derek's adventure during that big storm? This is Megan, his rescuer and heart-stealer."

"Well, she had the heart-stealer part down before my desperate attempt to get her attention by almost dying on her doorstep." Derek's lighthearted banter made the group laugh. Megan remembered something else she needed to ask Haven about. "I've officially adopted Dobby, the DK9 dropout. I hear there is a little girl to thank for his wonderful 'singing' ability?"

Haven buried her head in her hands. "I'm so sorry. Miah has so much fun with Dobby that weekend, I never imagined it would lead to that!"

Megan smiled, "It's perfectly fine. I can't wait to meet her and show her how Dobby's been adding some dancing to the routine. Is she here?"

"Not tonight," Jeremiah spoke up. "We needed a night on the town, so grandma is playing babysitter."

Derek chimed in, "We should get together and have dinner sometime soon."

After making plans with them, Derek and Megan moved across the room to grab some food. "I heard Van made some tiramisu for tonight. He's the pastry chef at Liberty Grille, and he will knock your socks off."

"I remember! I got the caramel apple cheesecake with room service while I was staying there. So good!"

They found a small table and took turns taking bites of the decadent coffee-laden dessert. Derek turned his piercing blue eyes on her and Megan felt her heart flutter.

"I'm glad you're here. I mean, I still kind of can't believe it, but I feel like the luckiest guy in the room."

Heat rose in her cheeks. "I feel the same way. I can't

think of a way I would rather kick off the new year than with you."

Jan sidled up to their small table with a proud look on her face. "Look at you two!" She turned to Megan. "I was worried when you wouldn't come to the wedding with him that Derek here had blown his chance. Turned out God's timing was better than mine. Who knew?" She delivered the last line with a laugh and Pete came up next to them as well.

"Glad to see you guys looking friendlier than the last time I saw you. Things were nearly as frosty inside my truck as outside in the remnants of the storm."

Megan laid her hand on Derek's arm. "Yes, we are all good. Thanks again, by the way, for everything you did to rescue us and set me up at the lodge."

"My pleasure. I do think I need to look into a whole house generator for some of my rental properties. Although, that was one doozy of a storm. They don't come around like that often."

The table chorused their agreement and Pete turned his attention to Jan. "You look lovely tonight, Janet.

Color rose in the older woman's face and she waved a hand. "Thanks, Petey. You look pretty dapper yourself."

The older couple was too cute, but Megan knew they'd swear there was nothing but an old friendship between them. Time would tell. And Megan was excited to realize that she would be here to witness it. This small town had become so much more than a writing retreat destination since she arrived three months ago. Against all odds, and despite her reluctance to open up, it had become home.

She tightened her grip on Derek's arm. "I love you," she said.

He glanced down at her with a grin. "I love you, too."

~

THEIR LIPS MET and Derek couldn't help but feel like the fireworks were already going off.

"Come on, you too, that's supposed to wait until midnight!" Derek looked up to see Dan and Ashley Winchester. "You've got," he checked his watch, "two more minutes."

He grinned at his friends. "Good to see you guys. Have you met Megan?"

Ashley shook her hand, "I think we met while you were staying at the Lodge over the holidays, right? I'm the chef at Liberty Grille."

Megan's eyes lit with recognition, "Oh, of course. I didn't recognize you without the white coat and hat," she joked.

Daniel and Ashley had gotten married this summer. With another glance at Megan, Derek couldn't help but wonder if next Christmas, they would be one of the newly wedded couples walking around with stars in their eyes. They didn't have the history like Max and Thea did, but he could understand Max's eagerness to tie the knot. There was nothing Derek wanted more than to proclaim to the world how much he loved Megan Warren and make her his forever. Megan was already looking for a place to live that allowed dogs so she could make good on her promise to Dobby.

For tonight, though, as the countdown started, Derek was more than content with taking her in his arms. Across the room, he saw Carson and Nicole wrapped in a similar embrace. Did he and Megan look as enamored as his buddy and his new wife? *Ten, nine, eight.* He looked into the brown eyes behind her glasses and smiled. *Seven, six.* Yes, he had a feeling the next year was going to be his favorite one yet. *Five, four.*

Starting the new year with a beautiful, strong, courageous woman by his side? *Three.* It wasn't what he had expected, but he wouldn't trade it for anything. *Two.* His heart thundered as he traced a finger down her smiling cheek. "I love you, Megan."

One.

With cheers and noisemakers erupting in the room, he captured her mouth under his and claimed the promise of a new year that would be unlike any other. He pulled her closer and molded their lips together in a searing kiss that chased away any chill from the wintry night outside.

"The fireworks are starting outside in two minutes!" Someone yelled over the crowd, and Derek pulled back from Megan, before dipping his head for one more taste.

"I love you, too," she whispered with a smile. "Happy New Year."

Indeed it was.

HAVE you read the rest of the Heroes of Freedom Ridge Series? Start at the beginning with Book One, Rescued by the Hero.

. . .

THE HARDEST PART **about this fake relationship is hiding it from her brother. Especially when it doesn't feel fake.**

∽

JOIN IN ALL the fun at our Facebook Reader Group
www.facebook.com/groups/freedomridgereaders
For sneak peeks, giveaways, and tons of Christmas
romance fun!

ACKNOWLEDGMENTS

First and Foremost, thank you, King Jesus. I am continually in awe of the countless blessings You've bestowed on me. May these words be a worthy offering!

To the readers, thank you for your kind notes and encouragement. For choosing my stories from a sea of options and continuing to do so with each new release.

To Hannah Jo Abbott and Mandi Blake, for being the best accountability, prayer, and venting partners a girl could ask for. This book seriously wouldn't have happened without you.

And to the rest of the Freedom Ridge authors – Elle E. Kay, Liwen Ho, and M.E. Weyerbacher. It has been an honor and a joy to work alongside you to create this world.

And to the rest of my Author squad -- Jess Mastorakos, Elizabeth Maddrey and K Leah. You guys make me a better writer, and I love our chats!

To Gabbi, who is still my biggest cheerleader and my favorite person to talk books with.

To my parents, for being a wonderful example of love, faith, and hard work.

To Carla and Jessica for encouragement, wisdom, and the occasional meal as I struggled through this season.

And finally, to my husband. I couldn't do this if it weren't for your willingness to take on bedtimes and guys' nights, and listen to all my rambling thoughts. I don't tell you enough how amazing you are.

Mr. B and Little C; Mommy loves you more than a million words can express.

HEROES OF FREEDOM RIDGE SERIES

(Year 1)

Rescued by the Hero (Aiden and Joanna)

Mandi Blake

Love Pact with the Hero (Jeremiah and Haven)

Liwen Y. Ho

(Year 2)

Healing the Hero (Daniel and Ashley)

Elle E. Kay

Stranded by the Hero (Carson and Nicole)

Hannah Jo Abbott

(Year 3)

Reunited with the Hero (Max and Thea)

M.E. Weyerbacher

Forgiven by the Hero (Derek and Megan)

Tara Grace Ericson

OTHER BOOKS BY TARA GRACE ERICSON

Main Street Minden Series

Falling on Main Street

Winter Wishes

Spring Fever

Summer to Remember

Kissing in the Kitchen (A Main Street Minden Novella)

The Bloom Sisters Series

Hoping for Hawthorne

A Date For Daisy

Poppy's Proposal

Lavender and Lace

Longing for Lily

ABOUT THE AUTHOR

Tara Grace Ericson lives in Missouri with her husband and two sons. She studied engineering and worked as an engineer for many years before embracing her creative side to become a full-time author. Now, she spends her days chasing her boys and writing books when she can.

She loves cooking, crocheting, and reading books by the dozen. Her writing partner is usually her black lab - Ruby - and a good cup of coffee or tea. Tara unashamedly watches Hallmark movies all winter long, even though they are predictable and cheesy. She loves a good "happily ever after" with an engaging love story. That's why Tara focuses on writing clean contemporary romance, with an emphasis on Christian faith and living. She wants to encourage her readers with stories of men and women who live out their faith in tough situations.

HOPING FOR HAWTHORNE

His sister's friend.

Her childhood crush.

All grown up.

Hawthorne Bloom is living for the moment, until a beautiful stranger with intriguingly familiar eyes gives him a tongue lashing he'll never forget. When she shows up again at a family event, Hawthorne finds himself trying to dig a way out of a hole he didn't realize he was in.

When Avery Chase returns to Indiana, the last thing she expects is to run into her childhood crush, let alone to realize in the years since she left, he's turned into a complete jerk. Hoping for a man to change is a mistake she's made once before and is determined not to make again.

Then again, it's hard to resist when your childhood crush finally notices you.

A sweet and clean, stand-alone Christian romance novella that will have you falling in love with the Bloom Family. Hoping for Hawthorne is Book 1 in the 7-book Bloom Sisters Series.

Made in United States
North Haven, CT
21 February 2022

16362943R00098